An Irresistible Shadow

KIRSTEN S. BLACKETER

An Irresistible Shadow
Book 1 in the Shadow Guardian Series

Copyright © 2013 Kirsten S. Blacketer.

This is a work of fiction. Similarities to real people, places, or events are entirely coincidental.

Printed in the United States of America.
Second Print, June 2015
ISBN: 978-1966905066

Cover Art: The Midnight Muse
Editor: Jayne Wolf

Written by Kirsten S. Blacketer.
Published by BlackShip Press
Kirsten.blacketer@gmail.com

https://kirstensblacketer.com

Dedication

Mom and Dad, thank you for fostering my love of the written word and believing that I had what it takes to be a writer.
My husband and my kids, who support me 100%, I love you.

The Sarcastic Muse Writers, you guys mean the world to me. To everyone who believed that I could do this…your kind words were always the push I needed.

And to the creators of Assassin's Creed…the catalyst for the inspiration for my Shadow Guardians. Thank you.

Table of Contents

Chapter One

England, Spring 1329

Evelyn turned to her cousin and dearest friend with a look of pure disbelief. "How could you say such a thing? Do not curse me so. You know how I feel about marriage and, perish the thought, love."

Madeline smiled at what Evelyn was sure was a scowl marring her brow. "You cannot avoid it forever. Most women of your age and station are married with bairns of their own."

She held her hand up as Evelyn opened her mouth to protest. "I realize it is not my place to say, but 'tis unseemly for a woman of your station to remain unmarried. I merely wish that you, my friend, are fortunate enough to find love. Many cannot afford such a luxury." Her hazel eyes glowed with hope for her cousin.

Evelyn sighed. "I have no use for an institution in which women are considered property." The thought of it paralyzed her with fear. *Perhaps I could marry an old man and hope for him to pass on quickly.* She shook her head at the wicked thought, but widowhood afforded her the only true chance at independence. She did not require a man to define her. The very thought of marriage made her sick with apprehension.

"Your father has given you the freedom to choose from the suitors," Madeline reminded her. "That is rare indeed. Despite your father's indulgence, even he would not leave you unprotected."

"Father is the only man I would trust to that degree. I am not sure I am fortunate enough to find another man as loyal or honest as he."

Madeline's laughter fueled her resolve.

"You laugh at me?"

"Your expression is so serious, Evey."

"If I were to marry, I would want a union such as my parents enjoyed." The Baron of Rayne and his Scottish bride had shared a love deeper than the differences in their ancestry. He had been devastated when she passed, leaving him with his young daughter. Madeline's arrival soon after was as much for Evelyn's sake as his promise to his late wife to care for her niece.

"I will think no more on marriage," she said with a toss of her head. "Caring for the people of this barony and planning father's coming Spring Tournament are more pressing concerns than marriage. By the by, I granted Rose leave to visit her family for a few days. Her sister just had a baby."

A natural leader, Evelyn was aware women were at a disadvantage. She made certain she kept informed of the concerns and politics of the region and often advised her father.

Madeline's reply passed unheard as Evelyn's thoughts turned to the constant turmoil churning on the border with the Scots. Sir Richard, self-styled advisor to the baron, pressed her father continually for a more aggressive stance against the wild northerners. Evelyn found Sir Richard's assessment of the Scots laughable. They were no different from the English, for all their pride in heritage and a desire to be independent. Her father always weighed his decisions carefully and knew the implications of becoming involved in such a struggle could be devastating. Still, Vile Richard, as she liked to call him, came close to ensnaring her father in his scheme.

"Evelyn." Madeline's voice broke her reverie.

"I beg your pardon. I have been woolgathering," Evelyn apologized.

Madeline offered a half smile. Evelyn saw she had more to say, but her feelings on the matter were quite set. The two moved in companionable silence as they carefully packed the herbal tinctures into straw filled boxes.

"Do not worry about me, Maddy," she said as they finished. "I shall be quite content without a man, you shall see." She nodded for emphasis.

Madeline shook her head and changed the subject. "Will you

take your afternoon stroll in the garden today? The rain has cleared."

"I believe you are correct." Evelyn caught a glimpse of sunlight streaming through the windows. "I think, perhaps, I shall take a ride through the glen instead."

"Your father always said you were born on horseback. You are going to abandon your escort again. Are you not, Evey? I can tell by the look on your face."

"I am capable of protecting myself, I thank you." On her tenth birthday, Evelyn, hands on her hips, demanded of her father a sword of her own. Although her father laughed at his wee daughter's request, he granted her private lessons in both archery and swordsmanship at which she excelled. Evelyn was more than capable of defending herself. Putting thought to deed, she tossed her apron on the table and strode from the room heading for the stables.

Madeline muttered something under her breath that sounded vaguely like spoiled.

The sun cast a halo of gold over the bailey. Evelyn ambled toward the stables, greeting everyone she met along the way. Several knights trained in the courtyard. She lingered to observe their practice.

The knights wore nothing but loose fitting linen shirts and leggings as they trained. Each of them drenched in sweat. Their finely honed physiques held her captive for a moment. It was inappropriate for her to see them thus, but whenever someone chastised her, she waved them off.

An unfamiliar face caught her attention. He was the new knight her father had mentioned, Sir Alexander.

He sparred with Sir Edward and, by the looks of it, was beating him with no apparent struggle. The two men were alike in stature, but the similarities ended there. Sir Alexander was dark where Sir Edward was fair. His hair, a deep rich mahogany, showed gold highlights in the sun and his skin was tanned. Although Evelyn could not clearly discern his facial features, she knew they would be dark and mysterious.

She observed his technique as he arced the broadsword,

bringing it metal to metal with his opponent's. He was like an avenging angel, or a roman god. Evelyn refused to let his appearance speak for him.

With one swift deft motion, Alexander relieved Edward of his sword. Both men nodded in acknowledgement. He extended his hand to help Edward to his feet and exited the ring as two younger knights began their round. He glanced at Evelyn briefly before dipping the ladle into the water bucket next to her. He lifted the cool water to his lips.

"Good day, Sir Alexander," Evelyn greeted him with a smile. "You handle that sword with exquisite skill." He gave her a curt nod.

She tried engaging him again. "I do not believe we have been introduced. I am Lady Evelyn."

His eyes captured her attention. They were not dark, as she had imagined, but an unexpected icy blue, framed with thick lashes under an arched brow. His gaze slipped from her face. She followed his line of sight. Madeline crossed the courtyard, heading toward the garden. He dropped his attention to the water bucket again.

"I know who you are." He swallowed another brimming ladle. She watched the muscles in his neck as he drank, then wiped his mouth with the back of his hand. Evelyn cleared her throat.

"Well then, since that formality is out of the way, I would like to welcome you to the barony." She worked to keep the rising irritation from her voice.

He gave a second curt tilt of his head, his attention focused on the two knights now sparring. She scowled. Every knight, even Richard, treated her with the respect due her station. Sir Alexander's blatant dismissal riled her. Though it was clear he did not think highly of her, she was determined to gain his respect.

"My father tells me you have just come from Scotland," she said, expecting a reaction. "You must have some interesting stories to tell."

His head snapped in her direction, his cold appraisal sent a shiver through her.

"Trust me, my lady." The words slipped from his lips in a disdainful hiss. "It would be unwise to interfere in business that is none of your concern." He looked away. "You should confine yourself to pursuits more suited to your gender and station."

Evelyn's blood boiled, her palms itching for the pommel of her sword. She bit her tongue and tried for a more subtle response than the curses filling her thoughts.

"Pardon me for *interfering* in your masculine duties," she replied, pasting a false smile on her face. Evelyn spun from him, spine straight, when his hand gripped her arm. She turned back, furious. "Unhand me, sir!" He did not release her.

"If you have any intention of leaving this keep, I strongly suggest that you take an escort. 'Tis not safe for you to be alone." A knowing look pierced her, causing her to bristle in defiance.

She jerked free of his grasp. "I am perfectly capable of taking care of myself, I thank you." She glared at him once more for good measure, then fumed all the way to the stables where her palfrey waited.

Alexander stared after the irate Lady Evelyn as she stomped into the stables. She was angry with him. *Good.* He did not want her getting involved; women always complicated things. *Best to keep her out of harm's way.*

Alexander grabbed his shirt from the fence and pulled it over his head. As he gathered the rest of his gear, his thoughts turned to an earlier confrontation. Sir Richard cornered Alexander in the hall with thinly veiled threats in an attempt to discourage him from speaking with the baron. While the action did not achieve its intended goal, it did grant Alexander a glimpse into Sir Richard's character.

The self-serving bastard deserved a good thrashing. Sir Richard, busy scheming for the baron to push the English into Scottish territory, did not comprehend Alexander was unmoved or he had just made a powerful enemy. The baron supported and protected the English crown, but he also respected the Scots desire for independence.

Alexander's mother had been Scottish. He had a moral duty to inform the baron of the serious implications of decrying the treaty between the two nations.

Alexander strode off in the direction of his lodgings. *Lady Evelyn.* She seemed sincere in her welcome, but he did not need nor desire her welcome. It was best for him to push her away. Her reaction to his insults told him he achieved his purpose. His mission was to protect her. She was the baron's only child and therefore a valuable asset. He watched her over the last few days. She was striking for a woman, tall and strong yet feminine and graceful. She was a singularly unique woman, well regarded and that meant she would not be ignored. His actions posed nothing but a challenge to her. His frowned deepened when he saw her ride out the postern gate. Alone.

"God's blood, stubborn woman!" he spat under his breath. He reversed direction, moving briskly toward the stables. Then he saw Lady Evelyn's cousin, Madeline, return from the gardens. Her red dress swished as she walked across the courtyard, a basket tucked under her arm. She cast him a sly glance, favoring him with a smile.

He had noticed her the day he arrived at the keep. Her hair was braided, framing her face in tight curls beside her head. Eyes bright and alert, they locked on him and followed as he made his way to report to the baron. In that moment, his mind strayed from his task and lingered on the angelic creature staring at him. Since then, he couldn't walk into a room without searching for her.

A high pitched whinny echoed through the courtyard. His gaze shot from Madeline to the stables just behind her where a stallion reared on his hind legs, pawing at the groom who struggled to control him. The line snapped and the horse jerked free of the boy's grasp. The stallion bolted, heading straight for Madeline.

Alexander sprang into action, fear clenching his heart. In

several swift strides, he was at her side and scooped her into his arms, turning his back to the charging beast. At the last second, the horse shifted course and ran out the main gate. A group of the guards blocked the horse's path, effectively stopping the destrier.

"Sir Alexander," a soft voice brought his attention to the woman he held against his chest. "You can put me down now."

He glanced at the woman in his arms. Her cheeks were flushed with a pink glow, mouth slightly parted as she studied his face.

"Aye," he said, gently lowering her feet to the ground.

"I thank you for saving me." Her smile sent a tremor of lust straight to his groin. He nodded as she walked to the great hall. Alexander shook his head and refocused his attention.

"Damn," he swore as he remembered why he had been headed for the stables in the first place. Lady Evelyn was probably long gone by now. Darting into the building, he grabbed his horse and walked back into the courtyard. He swung bareback onto his black destrier and followed Lady Evelyn through the postern gate. She was nothing but trouble and needed a shadow to keep her contained.

Sir Richard Langley watched the spirited Lady Evelyn ride through the rear gate, Sir Alexander following hard on her heels. *Interesting.* Sir Alexander was arguably the most honorable knight in the barony. Richard snorted. Power was a man's game, and Richard an experienced player. Why else would he banish himself to this backwoods barony to capture the ear of James Mongtomery, Baron of Rayne.

Richard's intention of raiding the brewery for a pint was pleasantly interrupted by the opportunity to gawk at the lady of the house. Heavens, but she was a succulent berry, ripe for the picking. Defiant and unconventional, the lady in question chose to wear her hair in a long plait, her head covered by little more than a scrap of linen. Her bearing and the way she sat a horse commanded respect. The Lady Evelyn was long past the day she should have been married to a man with a firm hand and saddled with brats. Someone needed to bring her into line, to show her skill with a sword alone did not make her equal to a man. Perhaps he should speak with the baron about his wayward child.

Richard gave up his quest for ale to search for Lady Evelyn's servant, Rose, the sudden need for companionship making him irritable. She would be leaving the keep the next day to visit her family. Perhaps he could entice her to spend the night with him. The memory of her soft curves and innocent demeanor made him hard. He slipped into the great hall. Several esteemed men of the baron's household sat discussing plans for the upcoming tournament. They glanced up from their good-natured squabbling to acknowledge his presence.

"Sir Richard, just the man we need," one of them called in a hearty tone. "Come join us. We need a strategist to aid us in finalizing these plans."

Steeling himself against a hasty and ill-thought reply, he put his hand up.

"Beg pardon, but I have urgent business to attend." The men nodded as he walked past them and headed for the baron's working chambers. So much for finding Rose, but this would be the perfect opportunity to speak with Evelyn's father and set his plans into motion.

He knocked on the door.

"Enter," the baron's voice boomed through the solid wood.

Richard pushed the door open and stepped inside the opulent chamber. Rich tapestries and dark wood filled the space. The Baron of Rayne sat behind his desk.

"Sir Richard. What can I do for you today?" he asked, leaning back in his chair.

"My lord, I have come to talk to you about your daughter." Richard chose his words carefully.

"Has something happened?"

"Nay, my lord," he replied. "However, I have come to ask what your plans are for her future. She is well beyond the age she should have married. 'Tis not seemly for a woman to be unmarried at her age. She needs a man to guide her, care for her." The baron rubbed his chin in thought. "I would like your blessing to court Lady Evelyn, my lord."

"Are you in earnest, Sir Richard?" The baron's eyebrows shot up in surprise. "I have never seen you take an interest in my daughter before."

"I have thought long and hard about this course and know that Lady Evelyn would make the perfect companion for me."

"You are aware of my daughter's thoughts on marriage?" the baron asked, searching Richard's face.

"Aye, my lord. But we both understand that she cannot remain unmarried and free to gallivant across the countryside on her own whims. For her safety, I beg you to consider my offer."

"I will think on it. I thank you for your concern." The baron returned to his paperwork as Richard bowed and left the chamber.

Grinning to himself, he headed to the kitchens to find Rose. He needed to relieve the ache in his loins. Somewhere inside his dark heart he wished Rose were Lady Evelyn and longed for the day he could take the spoiled bitch to his bed.

Bent low over the horse's neck, Evelyn spurred her horse into a gallop. The trees whipped past as the wind snatched the linen veil from her head, freeing curls from her coif. She reveled in the moment, exhilarated by freedom. A thrill shot through her as she dodged a low hanging branch then urged her gelding over a fallen tree. Horse and rider surged together as they hurtled through the forest.

Evelyn slowed the gelding to a walk, weaving deeper into the thickening underbrush. As the rush of her liberating ride drained away, her mind wandered back to Sir Alexander's appalling lack of respect. Only a brutish cur would insult a gracious welcome. Her horse sidestepped, and Evelyn shook free of her fuming. "My apologizes, Jester, 'tis not your fault." She patted his neck.

Twisting in the saddle, she surveyed her surroundings. Several hundred feet ahead, the trees opened into a small glen. She steered Jester toward it with a gentle nudge of her heel. The smell of wood smoke reached her as she approached the tiny cottage tucked into the back of the clearing. Eager to arrive at her destination, she trotted Jester along the tree line, welcoming happy memories of many previous visits.

While doctors and surgeons used torturous instruments and bloodletting to treat illness and wounds, Old Nora specialized in herbal cures. Nora, who taught Evelyn's nature-loving mother the secrets of herbal healing, took a young Evelyn under her wing giving her the same lessons in the art of herbal medicine. The noblewoman devoured the knowledge, finding a sense of purpose in helping others. When a band of brigands attacked the village last spring, Evelyn had helped Nora stitch wounds and apply salves. The women enjoyed each other's company, and Evelyn grasped every opportunity to visit her friend.

Nora's cottage sat in the part of the forest stretching between the village and the Scottish border, serving as a haven from politics and responsibility. Her heart yearned to stay with Nora, to ignore the harsh realities of her life. As she brought the gelding to a halt, Old Nora rounded the corner of her home.

"Evelyn, my dear, you have come to visit." The old woman's toothless smile was warm with welcome. She coughed, setting down her armful of wood. "Well, slide off that horse. Come keep an old woman company."

Evelyn stepped down from the saddle to tie Jester to the small fencepost and followed her surrogate mother into the warm cottage. Nora's home was sparsely furnished but held all the charm and comfort necessary to live a contented life. Bundles of dried herbs hung from the rafters, filling the room with their calm, soothing scents. Nora added some kindling to the fire. A pot hanging in the hearth emanated a savory aroma. Evelyn's stomach rumbled at the thought of a hearty meal. Old Nora had anticipated her arrival it seemed.

"Are you finding all the herbs you need this spring?" Evelyn asked as Nora added a few sprigs of mint to the stewpot.

"I have gathered as many as I can," Nora said. "Chicory is proving hard to find this year."

As she stirred the stew, a deep, hacking cough seized the frail woman, doubling her over in obvious pain. Evelyn rushed to her side.

"Are you well, Nora?" Evelyn asked, worried.

"'Tis naught but a spring chill, child." Nora brushed away her concern. "I shall be right as rain in a few days. You will see."

"How long have you been ill?" Nora had been quite well during their last visit, just two weeks prior.

The smaller woman yielded to Evelyn's persistent concern, settling herself into a chair and allowing Evelyn to wrap an extra shawl about her shoulders.

"I fear I might have taken ill with the same sickness as Benny Thatcher and his family. I had the whole family set to rights within a week. All these old bones need is some rest and herbs," she replied as a fond smile creased her cracked lips. "Do not worry about Old Nora, dear. Nothing keeps me down for long."

Evelyn ladled stew onto a trencher and set it before her friend. Nora looked as though she had aged ten years since her last visit. At Nora's urging, she served herself as well.

"What brings you out today?" Nora asked, taking a bite.

Evelyn broke off a piece of bread and dipped it into her stew.

"Well," she sighed, "Sir Richard has been pushing to cross the border in retaliation against the rebels. The peace is stretched thin enough as it is. I fear he may be manipulating father." She hesitated, not wanting to burden Nora while she was ill.

Nora nodded so Evelyn continued.

"I do not trust Sir Richard or his intentions," she said. "His primary interests seem to be wealth and power, and his ego has grown since he gained favor with my father. I fear he seeks to take advantage." She sighed, pushing bits of stew around with her knife. "Until last week, I thought Sir Richard might succeed in convincing my father to take action."

"Until last week? What happened? Did Richard finally *haud his wheesht*, or has your father kicked his pampered arse back to London?" Nora asked, a sarcastic twinkle in her grey eyes. Evelyn laughed at the thought.

"Nay, neither I am afraid, but a new knight has arrived. Father is listening to his experience with the Scots and the rebels. His extreme distaste for Richard is a point in his favor."

"Ah, this new knight may prove useful." Nora was thoughtful. She patted Evelyn's hand. "The baron is fortunate to have a daughter such as you to take an interest in such things. You have a new ally it seems."

"That remains to be seen. Though he has my father's ear, I find him rude and pompous." Evelyn shook her head, leaning back in her chair and crossing her arms.

Nora chuckled, raising an eyebrow.

"He loathes me," she huffed. "He is intolerable and insulting. I care for him not one whit." Evelyn nodded for emphasis.

"Still, he may prove helpful to you and your father. Keep him close."

Evelyn scoffed. She would rather die than keep such a man in her confidence.

"It grows dark, my child. You should return to the safety of the keep," Nora said, glancing out the small window.

"Thank you for the meal. I shall be back to see you within a few days." She hugged the frail woman. "Take care, my friend." Evelyn kissed her withered cheek and swung into the saddle.

Nora waved from the doorway. Evelyn smiled in return and urged Jester forward. As the sunlight faded into the trees, she nudged him into a canter, savoring her last moments of freedom before returning to the confines of her life.

The sun dipped low on the horizon, as Evelyn approached the outer walls of the keep. She dismounted and led Jester toward the postern gate. A patch of thistle blossomed near the stone barrier. She moved closer to gather some of the blooms, and then froze at the sound of voices. Silently tying the reins to a tree, she crept into the woods to hide in the underbrush. Two male voices reached her ears.

"I grow tired of waiting," the first man said with obvious irritation. "We should just kill him now."

Evelyn froze; dread lodging itself in her chest.

"Calm yourself. Stay close and be ready to move at a moment's notice. I will contact you when we are ready."

The undergrowth rustled as their footsteps receded from her, their voices fading into the distance. She backed out of her little hiding spot with care only to collide with a warm, solid body. A hand clamped over her mouth.

Chapter Two

Fear infused her body, Evelyn had been captured. The fear melted into anger. She thrashed in her captor's arms, twisting and kicking. His gloved hand tightened over her mouth and the other pinned her securely against his chest.

"I mean you no harm," a velvet voice whispered in her ear. "I do not want to bind you, but I will." Evelyn's heel connected with the man's shin. He cursed. "Although you evidently mean to harm me." His voice was calm, suffused with amusement. He carried her to where their horses were tethered.

Evelyn struggled to free herself, but he was much stronger. She was close enough to the keep to call for help, if he would only remove his hand from her mouth. He was all warm muscle against her back, a living, breathing stone wall. His breath caressed the fine hairs on her neck. When he stopped moving, she wedged her mouth open enough to fit her teeth around one of his fingers and bit down. Hard.

"God's blood, woman! I am trying to help you," he swore in his velvet whisper, then readjusted his hand over her mouth.

So much for that idea. If she had to play along with the rogue, so be it. He held no weapon to her throat. Though his hold on her was firm, he did not cause her pain. His muscles flexed as he shifted her in his grasp. She was keenly aware of every part of him that touched her. *Okay, so he had a weapon against me.* Though she had yet to see his face, her body betrayed her with its reaction. Evelyn inhaled in an effort to regain her composure and breathed in his scent. It was fresh, earthy, and dangerously sinful. She groaned, embarrassed by her wicked thoughts.

Her captor stilled, his breath quickening. "I will let you go," he murmured. "If you promise to behave." She nodded, relieved when he kept his word.

Evelyn broke from his embrace and spun on him. "Who are you?" she hissed. "What do you want?" She scrutinized the shadowed man before her. He wore all black: boots, leggings, tunic, and cloak. The hood covering his head was positioned low purposefully to hide his face from scrutiny.

The man proffered a sardonic bow, waving his arm with a flourish. "I am your humble servant, my lady."

The humor in his voice made her wary of his intent. "How did you know I was here?"

"I followed you," he answered.

She swallowed the lump in her throat. *Followed me?* The words of Sir Alexander echoed in her mind. She should have taken a guard. "Why did you not make your presence known?"

"That would not have served my purpose, my lady," he replied as he leaned against a tree, melding into the shadows. Since he seemed more amused than disturbed by her questions, she asked another.

"Why did you grab me?" she demanded, licking her dry lips. Formidable and mysterious, this man of the shadows aroused her curiosity.

"Ensuring your safety. You are not as quiet as you think you are."

Evelyn bristled. She was proud, unwilling to admit he was right. "Who do you think you are?" Her voice rose in pitch and fervor. "First, you follow me, then accost me, and finally insult me. You, sir, are playing a dangerous game. I should turn you over to the night watch." She poked him in the chest. "I do not need your help. I can take care of myself." Evelyn turned looking for her horse.

"I can see that," he said. She sniffed, ignoring his comment as she untied the reins.

"What did you overhear?" His velvet whisper was right next to her ear. She shivered, his voice a caress as it drifted over her shoulder.

She whirled on him, pushing him away. "I told you to stay away from me. What I heard is none of your concern!" Her mind spun with anger and shame at the desire igniting inside her like tinder at his touch. She pummeled her fists against his chest until she realized he had stopped backing away.

"Such fire, Princess," he chided. "Save your ire for when the fight is against someone you truly fear."

Evelyn froze. She did not fear him but hated being viewed as weak and helpless. *Does he know who I am?* She should be frightened, terrified that he would use her for his own gain. Her hands dropped as she chose a new plan of attack.

"So I am not to fear you?" she asked, setting her teeth in a feline smile.

He leaned close and whispered against her cheek. "Keep that smile on your face and you will have something to fear from me, Princess."

His nearness sent warmth thundering through her veins. His heat enveloped her. She searched the deep cowl for anything, even a glimpse of his lips, but the darkness allowed nothing. She closed her eyes in an effort to gather the thoughts swarming her mind like bees to a hive. It was unlike her to be rendered speechless by the very proximity of a man. But this faceless intruder had disabled her quick wit with nothing but a whisper. She inhaled. He was intoxicating. She glanced at him again, forcing herself to think beyond her attraction.

"I beg of you, release me," she murmured, weary of arguing with him. He backed away.

"Go home, Princess."

She gathered her horse's reins, knowing those unseen eyes followed her until she disappeared into the safety of the stone walls.

The shadow guardian watched as Lady Evelyn passed through the gate. As she vanished from sight, he exhaled unaware he had been holding his breath. Her scent of rosewater and the faint hint of horses dissipated into the dark as he stood there. He wanted her to turn and spout fire at him, wanted to see the passion blazing. Her unexpected retreat left him baffled. He knew her to be bright, intelligent, and spirited. She lit a fire of curiosity deep within his soul. If it was not already his mission to protect her, he would have done it anyway. Lady Evelyn was a rare jewel, and he would make sure nothing stole her brilliance.

This contradicted everything he had been trained to do. His job was to come and go without making contact, without revealing himself to anyone. The game only worked if he played it correctly. This passionate woman made him want to break the confines of his role. Although being a shadow gave him more freedom, it also made any attachments nearly impossible.

He wanted her. Not only because she was beautiful and the daughter of a prominent baron, but because she was fearless. She knew what she wanted. He had been monitoring her for a while and she never ceased to surprise him. Whether it was her cutting wit against the knights, or the sweet charm she used when speaking with the villagers. She proved herself a strong leader. He wanted her for his own, and that desire only grew since he had spoken to her.

How could he even contemplate breaking from the only life he had ever known for a woman? He shook his head, the conflict warring inside him.

He scanned the darkness. Though he had a responsibility as her guardian, he was late to meet with his informant. Moving with ease and stealth, he made his way to the stone wall. He slid along the wall and stumbled over a patch of thistles, snagging and ripping his leggings.

"God's blood," he muttered, trying to slip from the tangled mess of thorns.

"Who goes there?" A shout echoed over the wall. The shadow guardian forwent grace and silence, tearing himself from the brambles and darting into the forest.

He heard the guards approach and climbed into a tall oak tree to weave himself into the darkness. As they scoured the area beneath him, he cursed himself for being so distracted. Never had he allowed anything to affect his mission before.

Now he truly would be late for the rendezvous with his informant. *Damn it all!*

Evelyn slipped up the back stairs, hoping no one would see her. She wanted nothing more than to be left with her own thoughts. She had nearly gained the sanctuary of her chamber when she heard a voice behind her.

"Evelyn. I expected you back hours ago." Madeline stood, hands on her hips, as Evelyn turned around to face her. Madeline clucked like a disapproving mother hen.

"I am quite safe, as you can see. No need to worry." She pasted a smile on her face. "I was waylaid picking herbs in the glen and did not realize the hour had grown so late." Guilt washed over Evelyn for lying to her friend, but at the moment she craved peace.

Unpacified, Madeline touched her shoulder. "You were missed at dinner. I told your father you retired with a headache after your ride."

Evelyn smiled at her friend's resourcefulness. She would have been home in time for the evening meal had she not been stopped by the events outside the walls.

"Gra'mercy, Maddy. You are clever." She was grateful for her cousin's quick thinking. "I am tired. I believe I shall retire." Evelyn entered her chamber. "Goodnight, Madeline." She closed the door on Madeline's concerned frown. She did not have the energy to relay the evening's events, even to her dearest companion.

Besides, it would only lead to more guards, more rules, and less freedom. Madeline did not understand how the confines of the keep threatened to strangle her independent spirit. She could not bear to have any more restrictions placed upon her. She undressed down to her shift and wrapped a robe around her shoulders, glad of the warm embers glowing in the hearth.

Her visit to Old Nora had been routine enough, but she was concerned with her friend's health. She made a mental note to send provisions to the cottage the next day in the hopes it would ease Nora's burden. Perhaps Evelyn should invite the old woman to stay in the keep until she recovered her strength. She would send word in the morning.

She watched the embers glow and dance, her features pulled into a thoughtful frown. Evelyn tucked her knees up under her chin and wrapped her arms around her legs. Old Nora was not the only source of her anxiety. It began with her exchange of words with Sir Alexander. She had a solution to that problem readily enough: avoid him. If he would not provide her with information, let alone common courtesy, then she would simply talk to her father. He was always happy to include her in the affairs of the barony. With two problems solved, her thoughts turned to the last.

The conversation she overheard. A plot, and certainly one that would not benefit either the barony or the crown. Evelyn wanted more proof before informing her father. She had a good idea who was behind it, but she needed solid evidence. *Richard.* Even his name left a foul taste in her mouth.

Evelyn rose and crawled into her bed. She curled deep into the warm blankets, letting another image blossom in her mind. A tall, darkly garbed stranger stood inches from her, his soft soothing voice washing over her as he spoke. She swayed into him, feeling the warmth and strength of his body seep into her very core.

"Him," she whispered into the quilt. Evelyn did not want to observe this part of her evening too closely. She hated to admit it, even to herself, but she wanted to see him again, wanted to be near him and feel those same strange sensations that coursed through her body to do so once again. He was a danger to her, she could sense that. Never before had she desired a man or his company. That scared her more than death itself.

Evelyn tossed and turned under the blankets, her body restless. She stared at the ceiling. Admitting defeat, she rose and donned her robe. Perhaps a chamomile tea would help her sleep. She lit a candle in the dying coals and slipped down the stairs then across the small courtyard to the kitchens. Perhaps she would find something for her supper as well.

She set the kettle on the hook and poked the fire to life.

Evelyn reached up to retrieve sprigs of dried chamomile from the bunches drying in the rafters above her and dropped them into an earthenware mug. A bit of cold ham and pastry filled her belly as she waited for the water to heat. At last, with her mug filled, she took her candle and left the kitchen. As she closed the door behind her, an unwelcome voice interrupted her solitude.

"What are you doing?" Sir Alexander's disapproving gaze caught her unaware.

"I could ask you the same question," she said, refusing to be ruffled by his presence. His blue eyes seemed somehow warmer in the glow of the candle light.

"I heard a noise. 'Tis my duty to investigate."

"As you can see, 'tis only I. Now if you will pardon me..." Her gaze slid to the door behind him meaningfully.

He glanced at the mug in her hand and stepped aside. She brushed past him and hurried to the safe embrace of her chamber.

Evelyn closed the door with a sigh, setting her mug and candle on a small table by her bed. She added another log to the fire so it would not burn out before morning. The embers churned making it pop and crackle as the fresh logs smoked and burned. She sat for a moment in front of the hearth staring at the dancing flames, letting it lull her into a haze of contentment.

The scrape of leather on stone brought Evelyn to attention. She rose from her place by the hearth and silently backed into the shadows, groping for the sword she had left in the corner. Straining for the telltale sounds of movement, she heard only her shallow breath and the rapid beating of her heart. Her hand grasped at air, but the weight in her other hand reminded her of the poker dangling from her grasp.

Whoever dared to venture into her room was in for a surprise.

Chapter Three

Evelyn held her breath, waiting for the intruder to betray his location. The heavy drapes framing her balcony door had been left loose, providing a perfect spot to conceal oneself. She crept forward along the wall, her makeshift weapon poised to strike. The drape shifted. Her focus narrowed on the spot. Another rustle and she arched the poker in a downward strike.

The thunk of metal colliding with bone sent vibrations up her arm. The drape uttered a vile oath. Her instinct and training took over as she rained blows upon the man. The intruder stumbled from his hiding spot, arms shielding his face. Evelyn wielded her impromptu weapon in a well-aimed thrust, doubling the man over at the waist just in time for her overhand strike to catch him on the shoulder. He dove through the balcony door, pausing only to heft his weight over the railing, and disappeared faster than a rabbit chased by a hound.

Evelyn dropped her arms to her sides, a chilly breeze catching her shift. Pulling her robe around her, she stared into the dark garden. Her heart thundered in her chest. As her fighting reflexes abated, her body began to tremble. The severity of what just happened swept over Evelyn like a splash of cold water. Attacked, in her own room!

Who would dare to do such a thing? Anyone would have immediately assumed it was a Scot, coming to take vengeance on the English. With so much mixed blood in this barony, she doubted the Scottish would dare defy her father. She herself was half Scot; Madeline was full Scot, although most were unaware of that fact. It was still dangerous for them to assume any immunity. Rebels and mercenaries lingered on the border, waiting for opportune moments to stir up trouble. *Could it possibly be one of them?* They never worked without the promise of coin. Someone had to be controlling them. This had something to do with the meeting she overheard earlier.

She pressed her hands to her temple, then closed and locked the balcony doors. With a frustrated sigh, she dropped the poker and flopped onto the bed, burying her face in the coverlet. Her tears soaked the fabric. Although she was alone, she did not want anyone to see her cry.

The shadow guardian perched on the wall of the keep with an unobstructed view of the lady's chamber. When a shadow separated from the night to creep into the lady's boudoir, the guardian cursed softly. He dropped from his perch. It took him seconds to cross the garden and climb the section of wall outside of her room. He sat to the left of the balcony on a tiny ledge of stone and listened. The crackle of a fire and a feminine sigh met his straining ears.

Had his first impression been wrong? He had been confident of her innocence, the possibility she was attracted to him. The evidence of her inexperience showed when she attempted to flirt with him. Then again, the woman he thought of as a spoiled child was long past the time she should have been married. His shoulders slumped. Was there a reason for her unmarried state? She was beautiful and intelligent. Perhaps she entertained a lover? The thought of her enjoying a midnight tryst made his stomach churn.

The sudden thud and muttered curses propelled him to peek over the balcony railing. A defiant Evelyn wielded a fire poker against a hooded figure. Her perfect stance enlightened him to the extent of her training. The moonlight reflected the determination in her stance. She was glorious, hair loose about her shoulders, her white shift peeking through her bed robe.

Her attacker fumbled clear of the drape, arms flailing, desperate to protect his face and head, his dagger still tucked into his belt. The lady clearly had things under control. The intruder barreled through the doorway and over the railing. With a quick movement, the guardian ducked out of view as Evelyn approached.

Her face glowed in the moonlight, her riotous, dark hair backlit by the fire in the hearth. Her serious expression and readied poker would have looked ridiculous had it been any other woman. She was an avenging angel, a warrior princess. He moved further into the shadow as she closed and locked the door, but he did not leave. He thought he heard sobbing. The guardian sat in the shadows only able to wish her pain away. While in the distance, the shout of the guards echoed in the night. He grinned, glad the bastard had been caught otherwise he would have gone after the assailant himself.

Every sound, every whisper of wind made her jump. Her bed no longer offered the comfort she needed, and she was unable to focus on anything but the shadows created by the dancing flames in the hearth. Her tremors subsided as she focused on the details of the attack.

Dismay filled her. She had not seen the man's face, could not describe what he was wearing, could not even hazard a guess as to whether she had ever seen him before. Evelyn pinched the bridge of her nose. She should have raised the alarm, but the combination of instinct and delayed reaction held her captive in the aftermath. The intruder had vanished from her window like a shadow disintegrating into the night.

Shadow...was that not the same term she associated with the mysterious stranger whose husky voice made her shiver? Surely, he was not the intruder. *Nay*. The man she fought lacked the height and breadth of the man in the forest. The guardian was courtly, perhaps a knight of some kind. His cultured words hinted of intelligence and wit. Her body warmed. This yearning to know more about him was dangerous, but her heart begged to see him again. It was best to bury that desire in the depths of her mind.

As the flames died to embers, smoldering to coals, Evelyn

conceded sleep would not find her. She crawled from the warmth of her bed, located her sword, and padded down the hall to Madeline's bedchamber. Moving silently, she eased the door open and headed for the chair in front of the hearth. She curled up there, tucked her robe around her feet, and watched the shadows. She drifted to sleep, soothed by the rhythmic breathing of another living soul just as the bright fingers of dawn painted the sky.

The last remnants of sleep faded as Evelyn stirred. She stretched, arching her back and lifting her arms over her head. The memory of the attack slammed into the forefront of her mind. She bolted upright, nearly colliding with her cousin, who sat on the bed next to her.

"All is well, Evey." Madeline comforted her. Evelyn's heart slowed as confusion faded.

"How did I..." she began, then hesitated, flinching against the sunlight. "What is the hour?"

"Nearly midday, and I am most curious as to how you came to be curled up asleep in my room." She smiled.

Evelyn's cheeks warmed. Not wishing to discuss the previous night's events, she improvised.

"I had a nightmare and could not settle back to sleep," she said, relieved to see Madeline's expression soften. She was grateful her cousin did not mention the sword she had cradled as she slept. It rested against the wall next to her bed.

"Next time," Madeline said, "you can join me in the bed. That chair is terribly uncomfortable." She bustled about, opening the balcony curtains.

"How did I get in my own bed?" she asked.

"Oh, Sir Alexander happened by when I walked down to the kitchens. He offered his assistance." Madeline smiled.

"Madeline! How could you allow him to take such a liberty with my person?" The heat rose to her cheeks at the thought of

Sir Alexander's hands on her. Her cheeks grew hotter, drawing a laugh from Madeline.

"Och, Evey. All he did was carry you the short distance from my chamber to yours. I assure you, he took no liberties." Her explanation did nothing to ease the embarrassment consuming Evelyn.

Evelyn swept the bedclothes aside and changed the subject. "Help me dress, please. I have no time to lie about. Have you seen Rose? She has been absent forever, it seems."

"You gave her several days to visit her family, remember? I am sure she will return within a fortnight. She does have a tendency to be flighty." Madeline shook her head.

"Aye, that is true." Rose was a sweet girl with a pretty face; perhaps she caught the attention of a young man and forgot herself. Still, Evelyn was a tad concerned for Rose's welfare. She had been seen flirting with Sir Richard. Evelyn shuddered at the thought. She should warn the girl of his less than regal reputation.

Pushing the thought from her mind, her mood brightened as she dressed. She wanted to see her father, hoping he could provide her mind with a suitable distraction more productive than dwelling on the attack, or her injured pride.

"Good morrow, Father." Evelyn's cheerful tone and bright smile chased the silence from the baron's work chamber. Glancing up from the parchment before him, James Montgomery, the Baron of Rayne, watched his daughter enter. She wore a lovely russet gown, her bright green eyes belying the dark smudges underneath them. Sunlight streamed in through the open window, casting a glow on his only child, delicately highlighting her beauty. He was struck as always by her resemblance to his wild Scottish lass. In that moment, he realized his little girl had blossomed into a vivacious young woman. A twinge of regret stabbed his breast as she leaned down, pressing a kiss on his unshaved cheek.

His thoughtful gaze followed her as she idly perused the letters and missives littering his desk. She was willing to aid the people of the barony and concern herself with their wellbeing. He always included her in his decision making process. The tension along the border did nothing to make life easier for the girl who inherited more responsibility than should be placed on a motherless child. Though he was proud of her accomplishments, his concern for her future pulled the corners of his mouth downward. Maybe it was time to see her settled. Perhaps he should consider Sir Richard's request.

"Is something wrong, Father?" she asked, a crease marring her delicate brow.

"Nothing, my dear," he replied with a shake of his head. "You look fetching this day. What have you planned?" He gestured for her to sit as he leaned back in his chair.

"I was hoping you had some work for me," Evelyn replied, laying aside the parchment she had been reading.

"I have no pressing matters that require your attention today, daughter. But if I find something, you shall be summoned straight away." Evelyn smiled, but it failed to reach her eyes. "What ails you? Are you well?"

"Is Sir Richard still...I mean; is he still adamant in his pursuit of the Scottish rebels?"

"Aye, he is," the baron frowned. "I have not gathered enough information to make a decision yet. 'Tis an extremely delicate matter, one that I must investigate thoroughly before taking action. Sir Richard advocates for it, but there are those who oppose it."

"Sir Alexander." His name whispered off her lips, echoing with a hint of disgust.

"Aye, he is a valuable asset in that regard. His knowledge of the violence on the border is illuminating. He served the Crown valiantly, even after the loss of his brother. I believe Sir Alexander has proven his worth as a warrior, courtier, and politician."

"Perhaps." Evelyn hesitated, then continued. "Though he

shows me little respect or chivalry." Her mouth pulled into a pretty pout as she seated herself on a nearby bench.

The baron lay an affectionate hand on her knee. "Are you certain 'tis not your perception? I have seen no such behavior from him."

"I believe he disapproves of me."

"He does not know you as we do, my dear. You are a rare jewel. Give him time to recognize you for the asset you are." Perhaps the answer to his concerns lay with this new knight who captured his daughter's attention. He would much rather see her settled with a man like Sir Alexander than Sir Richard. He would foster this new interest in Sir Alexander.

"Perhaps."

"Sir Alexander is no stranger to progress. Time is your ally. Now, out with you. Let the sun bring some color back to your cheeks."

Evelyn rose and kissed her father's brow. "I believe I shall."

The baron watched her leave with a swish of her skirts. Time, indeed. He needed to make a decision concerning his daughter's future. Perhaps he should grant Sir Richard's request to court her. He would much rather encourage Sir Alexander to pursue his daughter. Evelyn would balk at the notion of marriage to either man, but perhaps she would come to accept him given the proper motivation. The baron glanced heavenward and sighed. "What am I to do with her, Rosalind? How I wish you were here to help guide her."

Shaking the fancy away, the baron refocused his attention to the papers before him. He silently prayed everything would fall into place, but deep down he already knew he might have to eventually break his daughter's heart.

Chapter Four

Evelyn closed her chamber door and slumped against it, fighting tears. She braced her trembling hand on the wall. Fury and disbelief knotted her stomach. She threw herself across the foot of her bed, burying her face in the soft bedcover.

Her day started well enough, and tea in the gardens with Madeline was lovely. When she stopped in the courtyard to observe the knights at practice, they avoided her. Composure intact, she had turned away, only to confront Sir Alexander's cool, blue scrutiny. Head high, she had brushed past him. At the evening meal, she sensed their stares and heard whispered conversations that disintegrated when she moved within earshot. Evelyn speculated she was the subject of their hushed comments, but could not fathom the reason.

She cursed heavenward. Life would have been infinitely easier had she been born a boy. All she wanted was the freedom to do and be what she desired. Damn tradition! Her father had supported her desire for independence for so long, but now it seemed that too had changed. He dropped a delicate hint at the evening meal he wanted her settled with a husband by summer's end. Instead of bristling in defense, Evelyn assured him she would take his advice into consideration. What pushed her over the edge was his suggestion she consider Richard as a suitor. She took the moment to excuse herself from the table and retreat to her room to rage in private.

She screamed into her coverlet, allowing the anger to vent. After she spent most of her ire, a soft shuffling sound reached her ears. She sat up quickly and scanned the room. The sound echoed again.

"Who's there?" Evelyn rose from the bed as her curtain wavered. No breeze touched it. She kept the balcony door closed after the attack. Perhaps Madeline had opened it to air the room. A shadow flickered behind the curtain. She carefully pushed it back. Nothing. Her reflection in the glass stared back at her.

The fading sunlight warmed her room with hues of amber and gold. Returning her gaze to her bed, she stilled. A single, fully blossomed scarlet rose lay upon her pillow. The perfect flower enchanted her. She plucked it from the linen to lift it to her nose, all concerns forgotten for one brief moment. The sweet aroma wove into her senses.

"Did you miss me, Princess?"

The serenity of the moment shattered. Evelyn spun toward the voice. A figure, shrouded in black, stood an arm's length away. He smelled nearly as good as the rose, a mixture of horses, leather, and the unmistakable hint of masculinity that was uniquely his own. The fading twilight illuminated the hooded man from behind, casting his features into shadow. She backed away slowly, pointing the rose at him as if it were a dagger.

"What do you speak of?" she asked, bursting the tiny bubble of excitement that formed in her breast at seeing him again. Her bottom slammed against the bed's edge. Evelyn tilted her chin up, searching the darkened cowl for eyes to pierce with her own.

The dark figure chuckled, lifting his hand toward her. She swatted it with the rose stem. With one fluid twist of his hand, he caught the stem in his fist. She ripped it from his grip, examining the perfect flower for damage. The stem shone with tiny red droplets, and several of the thorns were missing. Evelyn had drawn first blood. Guilt and anger flooded her body.

"Can you not just leave me alone?" she spat at him.

"You are quite comely when you are angry, but your smile is as radiant as a summer sunrise." Each word was spoken with a soft sensuality, making her shiver.

I have not smiled since I visited Nora. Her first encounter with him flashed into her mind. Had he been watching her the whole time? She dropped her gaze to the floor, a tell-tale burn of a blush ignited in her cheeks. She hoped the waning light hid it well.

"What is it you want from me?"

"I am a Shadow Guardian." He leaned toward her. "My purpose is to protect you from harm, even if it means protecting you from yourself." His voice was velvet soft.

"Who holds your allegiance?"

"You, Princess," he responded.

"You can address me with my proper title," she admonished, throwing the ruined flower to the floor to grind it beneath her slipper.

"You are not angry." He took a step closer. It was a statement, not a question.

"Aye, but I am," she said, setting her jaw and boldly glaring at him. "I do not need you to watch over me like a child. I can take care of myself." Her heart whispered a plea to accept him, trust him. Her pride fought back, sending her heart to a dark place deep inside. Her spine straightened. She refused to like this man.

"Forgive my intrusion," he bowed stiffly. "Fare you well, my lady." A chill embraced her as he stepped away. Her heart cried out, begging to give him a chance.

"And if I should require your assistance?" she murmured just above a whisper.

His hand hovered on the balcony door handle. "I shall be close by, hiding in the shadows." His reply was soft, as if to soothe her pride.

"Do you have a name, Shadow Guardian?" The question spilled from her lips before she could stop it.

His head turned towards her, face hidden deep in the hood, but the smile in his voice was clear.

"Gabriel."

With two swift strides, he disappeared over the balcony and into the waiting darkness.

The darkened chamber that housed his belongings was his refuge. Richard, frustrated with the day's events, slammed the door behind him. Sir Alexander proved to be a persistent thorn in his side. He needed relief. There was no way he could get it here without alerting suspicions. He slipped a cloak around his shoulders and glanced at his reflection in the mirror.

His black hair hung loose, framing his strong jaw. The firelight drew attention to the wicked gleam in his green eyes. He smoothed the hair back from his face, offering his reflection a grin. He tucked a dagger into his belt and left to find comfort where he could be uninhibited.

Richard pushed his horse faster through the thickening darkness. The moon hidden by the clouds made him reckless, desperate even. His destination lay just beyond the hills along the border. When he arrived at the tiny cottage, he tied his horse to the post and pushed hard against the door, swinging it open. She was as he had left her.

The woman scrambled to her feet, clawing at the wall, the chains dragging across the musty dirt floor. Her long hair hung down, covering her thinly clad, half-starved body. Her terror-filled gray eyes peeked between straggly, unkempt locks.

"Finding your accommodations adequate, pet?" he asked, closing the door behind him. He bent to stoke the fire, aware of her fearful gaze following his every move.

He rose and closed the gap between them with several swift strides. She slammed herself back against the wall, arching away from his touch. Richard brushed a rope-like strand of hair away from her face. She bit her lip and cringed when he slid his hand down her neck, over her shoulder, curving across her breast. He thrust his knee between her thighs, pressing her body between his and the wall.

"This is your own fault," he said. Grasping her chin, he snapped her head to face him. "Running to the old woman sealed her fate and yours." He slid his other hand beneath her shredded gown, rubbing against the soft folds between her legs. She whimpered as a tear escaped from under her lowered lashes.

He dropped his hands and stepped back. The girl collapsed in a heap on the floor, burying her face in her hands as she wept.

"Because of you, I was required to pay a visit to the old hag." He turned back to the fire. "Fortunately, you chose not to give her the name of your paramour. That might have jeopardized my plans." He glared at the crumpled wench. He had snatched her up after she ran to the old woman for help and hid her in this abandoned cottage. It had been an impulsive move that could spoil his plans. But he took care of all the loose ends, first Nora and now the deflowered Rose.

She whimpered, her body trembling.

"It was really no trouble to make her death look as if it was the Lord's plan." A sneer sprouted on his lips. "Though we both know *He* had nothing to do with it. Just a slip of foxglove in her stew and no one is the wiser. Except you, Rose."

He grabbed the chain off the ground and jerked the frail woman to her feet, tossing her on the bed. Richard unbuckled the belt at his waist, dropping it to the floor. As his fingers worked the buttons on his doublet, he appraised her cowering form.

"And I will make sure that you never speak to anyone ever again."

The next morning Evelyn left the keep on horseback before the sun broke the horizon. Sleep had evaded her completely the previous night. He filled her thoughts. His husky voice echoed in her memory. She shivered remembering the way his presence overwhelmed her. She had been rude, dismissing him with her words and actions even though he treated her with respect. Even his teasing comments had been respectful. He seemed genuinely concerned for her well-being. Her behavior had been thoroughly unforgivable; thinking about it left her both brooding and sad.

He is a man, Evelyn. All men treated women as if they were property, believing them subordinate to a man's will with no opinion or rights of their own. *Did they not?* With a shake of her head, she returned her focus to the trail before her. The sun beamed through the trees, surrounding her in comforting warmth. She pushed the hood from her head, basking in the spring sunshine.

Evelyn urged Jester onward, winding deeper into the forest.

Perhaps Nora would have some advice for her. She debated on whether to tell Nora about the strange shadow who had attached himself to her. The clearing came into view. As Evelyn glimpsed the cottage across the field, her instinct warned her something was not right. No smoke billowed from the small chimney. The silence made her uneasy. She kicked her horse into a slow lope, closing the gap to her friend's home. It had been only days since she had sent a guard with some provisions for Nora. She regretted not being able to deliver them herself, but plans for the tournament had kept her busy.

Upon reaching the cottage, Evelyn flung herself from the saddle and dropped the reins. She knocked several times and waited a moment before trying the handle. The door swung open, the interior dark and cold. She entered and searched the small space. The cottage looked the same as it had been upon her last visit. Perhaps Nora decided to check on one of her patients and had yet to return. It was common for her to be away for several days if the patient needed constant care. Evelyn touched her hand to the hearth stones, their chill confirming Nora's prolonged absence. A shiver of unease drifted through her, settling in her bones. She mounted her horse and left the clearing at a canter.

Just outside the village, Evelyn spied a boy carrying firewood. He turned his dirt smudged face up at her.

"I beg your pardon," she began, "I wonder if you might aid me in locating a friend."

"Who ya lookin' for?" he asked.

"Do you know the old woman, Nora, who lives in the clearing beyond those trees?" She pointed in the direction she had just come.

"Aye, she helps people when they are sickly." He looked down, a shadow touching his features.

"Do you happen to know if she is in the village? I was just to her cottage, and—" The boy cut her off.

"Begging pardon, my lady. She is not there anymore. Ma said she went to be with the angels. Said she fell asleep and never woke up." His voice was sad. "A crofter found her yesterday when he went to fix her roof."

Evelyn's heart sank to the pit of her stomach. *Dead?* Surely, there was some mistake. One look at the boy's face and she knew he spoke the truth. As she left the village, a riot of emotions bombarded her: shock, anger, disbelief, and fathomless despair. Evelyn remembered how frail and sick her friend had been a few days ago. Was it possible that she just slipped into eternal slumber? At least she had not suffered, but how she wished she had been there for her friend in her last moments. Evelyn shivered at the thought of dying alone.

Tears trickled silently down her face as she rode home, lost in memories of Old Nora and all they had shared.

Hidden by the thick forest trees, Gabriel sat easy in the saddle as Evelyn rode past. The glorious warrior princess he had come to admire slumped low, tears crisscrossing her pink cheeks. He did not presume to know her innermost thoughts, but it troubled him to see her bowed and broken in grief.

He had been following her since her pre-dawn departure from the keep, maintaining distance and shadow between them so she might remain unaware of his presence. A knot formed in his gut as she approached the empty cottage. He had known she was friends with the old woman. He wished he had told her, should have prepared her for what she discovered for herself in the last few hours.

Gabriel twisted in his saddle, reaching for his flagon. He took a healthy swallow and waited for Evelyn to come out of the cottage. While Evelyn remained inside the safety of the keep during the day, Gabriel scouted the barony on the border. Part of his mission was to know who and what moved through the area. Surprises were never welcome. He had heard of the old woman's death the day before, but hesitated to tell the Evelyn last evening. Gabriel watched Evelyn when she emerged from the house and mounted her horse. He noted the worried expression on her face as she kicked her horse into a swift canter, heading toward the nearest village. He kept to the forest shadows and observed her brief conversation with the woodcutter's son before slipping away to his present location.

He should have warned her.

His mission was to guard her with his life. Whether she approved of his presence or wanted his help proved a moot point. Her horse ambled down the dirt road. He longed to bridge the silent gap between them.

She made her desire to be left alone clear during their last conversation. Her ardent hatred for the patriarchal society poisoned her ability to be rational. When she finally found a way around it without open defiance, then the world would see what he already saw...her true value.

The garden lay eerie and quiet. The sound of her boots crunching down the stone path broke the silence. This was her favorite place, with its ethereal quality. The blooms blanketed the uneven landscaped greens. The small garden inside the keep had been a gift to Evelyn's mother from her devoted husband. Nature and a vast variety of flora and fauna came together creating a fragrant haven. What had been a passion for her mother now become the same for her. Evelyn sighed as she sank onto the bench next to the rose arbor concealing the garden gate, the postern gate lay beyond. She smiled at the memory of sitting in this very spot with Madeline, eagerly eavesdropping as the guards told bawdy stories.

The tears returned, slowly dripping onto her dress. Old Nora loved this garden. Her beloved haven would serve as a memorial to both her mother and her friend. Her heart ached. Letting go was always a hard lesson to embrace.

Evelyn missed the old woman's comforting voice. She lay across the weathered stone bench, draping an arm across her face. Footsteps approaching the garden from the postern gatehouse broke the silence. She sat up, dabbing her cheeks with her sleeve. *Must be Madeline coming to fetch me.* Evelyn stood, straightening her dress. As she reached for the garden gate, a man's voice rumbled through the vines.

"About bloody time you showed up." A low curse filtered through the roses. Evelyn froze, stunned. Was someone talking to her? *How rude!* She opened her mouth to reply when another man's voice left the words dead on her lips.

"I had to piss. Damn jakes are on the other side of the bailey."

Evelyn hesitated, leaning into the shadows of the bushes. Their voices sounded vaguely familiar. She held her breath.

"Do you have the message?" the first man groused, agitated and in an obvious hurry to be gone.

"Aye, on the morrow at the old Scottish abbey over the border, we shall get further instructions."

Evelyn held her breath, listening to the hurried conversation. *What luck! These men are the same I overheard the night I met...*she cut off the thought. This time there was no meddling shadow to snatch her away before she heard details.

"Get out of here before the guard returns," the second man said, his voice low.

Footsteps faded, leaving silence in their wake. Evelyn released the breath she had been holding and disentangled herself from the rose briars. A few scratches and snagged fabric were worth the information she garnered. Evelyn pushed her sadness away, allowing a sense of purpose to fill the void. She would unmask these villains, and perhaps secure her future freedom by proving she was more than just a pretty prize.

Alexander stood inside the postern gatehouse, tapping his foot with impatience. The changing of the guard would take place soon and he still had one more round to make before then. He took his duties seriously, but a man could only stretch himself so far before he broke. He would have made the rendezvous for later in the night, but he did not want to miss the evening meal. She would be there, providing the only bright spot in his day. Thinking about Madeline made his lips quirk up at the corners.

"Are you...smiling?" An amused voice teased from the shadows behind him. Alexander turned around slowly. Of course, he was hiding in the shadows. That is what he was supposed to do.

"You are." The surprised voice continued. "Well, well, well. You are not made of stone after all. Who is she?"

"Enough," said Alexander through clenched teeth. "Did you get any information?"

The shadows materialized into a figure before Alexander, his black garb blending into the night with a cowl covering his head.

"Nay," the shadow guardian said, disappointment evident in his voice. "But Lady Evelyn knows I am watching her. I doubt she will stray again."

A rough sound, almost a chuckle, burst from Alexander's lips. "Are you so certain?" he asked. "She is not the kind to take an order and sit meekly in the house. Keep a close eye on her when she leaves these walls. The Scots are aware of the English dissenters who wish to push the border north. They might grow desperate."

The shadow guardian laughed. "She has spirit. I will grant her that."

"Just watch her and be on the lookout for any unusual activity, and..." The sound of footsteps coming from outside the gate stilled Alexander's tongue. He pushed himself and the shadow guardian back into the alcove behind the gatehouse. They stood still as statues.

A man walked inside the gate and waited just outside the garden. He paused there a few moments, his agitation growing with every passing minute. Finally, another man approached him from inside the keep.

""Tis about bloody time you showed up," the outsider said.

"I had to take a piss," came the reply from the inside man.

Alexander and the guardian listened to the men, until they split, retreating in the directions from which they both came. Alexander looked at the guardian. "The old abbey? Perfect."

"The king had been right to send us. It seems unlikely Baron Rayne would strike at lowlanders who were once his neighbors without provocation. I will keep a close watch over Lady Evelyn," the shadow guardian said. "You remain close to the baron. Whoever is behind this has to be someone close to him."

Alexander nodded as his partner was engulfed by the shadows once again. He glanced up at the clear night sky. *Time to find out who lurks behind these treacherous games and prevent any hasty political decisions.* Trouble was brewing in the little barony on the border.

Chapter Five

Evelyn ventured toward her chamber after the evening meal. Her head spun with the information she had overheard earlier in the garden. Something had to be done. She hesitated to tell her father of what she discovered without proof. The identities of the traitors would be essential to unravel this devious plot. Was there anyone she could trust?

His name sprang unbidden to her mind. *Gabriel. But can I place my trust in him? More importantly, am I ready to trust him?* He had shown himself to be honorable and maintained his only goal was to keep her safe. If she included him in this scheme, she would have a partner and ally if her plans went awry.

It had one flaw, an element she could not control. Her attraction to Gabriel. His voice was a soft caress, causing a shiver of desire to trickle over her even now. She wondered why he kept his face in shadow. A device to hide his identity or was he horribly disfigured? Hideous or not, his presence brought unfamiliar sensations to life within her. She admired his quick wit and intelligence. She decided it would be unwise to underestimate him. Her breath quickened at the thought of spending more time with him. Curse her traitorous body.

Laughter floated down the hall behind her. She glanced over her shoulder, searching the empty corridor. She stepped blindly around a corner and collided with a solid wall of muscle.

"Sir Alexander," she gasped, taking a hasty step back, her gaze fixed on his.

"Pardon, my lady." He stepped to the side, allowing her to pass.

His gaze never wavered. This man was a confounding mystery to her. The perfect paragon of a courtly knight, but devoid of any human emotion, as far as at she could tell. She studied his cool stare.

"You do not care for me much do you, Sir Alexander?" she

said, a sly smile tugging at her lips.

"My lady?" he asked. She caught the flicker of amusement in his expression.

She leaned in conspiratorially. "I see the way you look at me, disapproving of my pastimes, my freedom." She paused, thoughtful. "Not many approve of my freedoms, but no one dare show their disdain for it, until you."

Unblinking, he stood watching her as silence descended on them. She smiled, adding her own observation as an afterthought. "I see the way you look at Madeline too."

His eyes widened. Not much, but enough to confirm her suspicions. A delicious shiver coursed through her as she teased the stoic knight, like poking a sleeping bear in his den.

"I am unaware to what you refer, my lady," he replied. "Pardon." Breaking the contact, he brushed past her, his heavy steps echoing down the hall.

At that moment, Madeline approached Evelyn from the direction Sir Alexander had come. Her words fell on deaf ears for Evelyn was lost in deciphering her conversation with the knight.

As Madeline continued, mentioning something about the tournament, Evelyn noted Sir Alexander's eyes had betrayed him. A heart truly did exist inside that man, as well as a cavern of secrets. *And I will fetch them out. Every. Last. One.*

Kindly excusing herself, Evelyn noticed Madeline's arched brow and pursed lips as she slipped into her chamber and readied for bed. While she hated to be rude to her cousin, there were larger things at play in the barony than a tournament.

She made a sleeping draught of chamomile to calm the racing thoughts in her head and ease her into a peaceful sleep. The conspirators' meeting was to take place the next day and she preferred to be fully rested for her first foray into espionage. Doubt still lingered. Should she enlist the aid of the mysterious Gabriel? As much as she longed for his company, her head condemned her for even considering him as a partner.

She brought the draught to her lips, draining the contents before returning it to the table. As she climbed into her bed,

Evelyn nestled under the covers and savored the warmth.

Her lids grew heavy as the herbs began their potent wonders. Her last waking thought was of the shadow guardian. As her body drifted into slumber, he followed her there, his velvet voice seducing her in her dreams.

The moonlight spilled through the balcony door as Gabriel slipped into Evelyn's chamber. The fire smoldered to glowing embers in the hearth. A slight breeze followed him into the room. He glimpsed his reflection in the mirror sitting on the mantle. A shadow of a man returned his gaze.

Gabriel frowned. This masquerade afforded him the pleasure of anonymity, but it also shrouded him in secrecy and deceit. He approached her sleeping form and his breath caught. *I should not be here.* His duty was to protect her, not invade her personal domain. While his head told him to turn and leave, his heart drew him to the woman before him.

She lay sprawled across the bed, a thin coverlet twisting around her legs and up her body. Her arms thrown wide, framing her sable curls as they fanned over the pillow. Deep in the embrace of sleep, she looked ethereal, peaceful. Her pale skin glowed in the moonlight as it spilled over her.

His shadow blanketed her when he leaned over. He pulled the glove from his hand and reached out, letting it hover over her. *This is wrong. Leave, damn you.* His body revolted as his fingertips touched the soft curls next to her cheek, brushing over her skin. She moaned, turning her face into the warmth of his hand. His palm cupped her face as he traced his thumb over her lower lip. Her mouth curved into a smile. The stolen moment was worth breaking all the rules.

"Gabriel," she sighed. He froze, afraid he had awakened her. She lay there, peaceful in sleep as silence descended on the room again. He removed his hand slowly, savoring the feel of her. His decision to come to her room had been reckless, but she enchanted him. Her allure called to him as he sat outside the keep. He could not deny his attraction to this woman.

He needed to leave before she woke. His heart pulled him into this room, while his mind raged against it. He had a duty to king and country, but what he really wanted was bathed in moonlight, dreaming of him.

With a soft curse, he turned from her and strode out the balcony door, disappearing into the night.

Evelyn prepared for her day, allowing a warm spring breeze to drift in through the open balcony door. She chose a sturdy working gown of earthen tones and braided her hair in a loose chignon. Since her maid had left, Madeline had been helping her dress. But this morning, she dressed herself. This day she would obtain the information she needed to bring down the traitors, whoever they might be. She cast a smile at her reflection, then turned and bounded down to the solar where she normally broke her fast with Madeline.

"Good morrow, dear cousin," Evelyn said with a smile.

Madeline glanced up so quickly she nearly overturned her full teacup. "Why are you so lively this morning?" Madeline gave her a wary glance. "You abhor mornings."

"Is that any way to greet your closest and most dear friend on this lovely day?" Evelyn refused to let her mood be dampened. "Can I not rise early to enjoy the beautiful sunrise and my cousin's company?"

Madeline's expression looked as though she had seen a pig sprout wings and fly past the window. "I suppose. Though you are certain to deny it, I sense a scheme brewing in that head of yours." She poured Evelyn a cup of tea.

"'Tis a fine day, is it not, Madeline?"

"You have already said as much," Madeline replied. "What are you up to?" She searched Evelyn with a wary look.

Evelyn picked up the hot beverage and sipped it carefully.

"I was hoping to take a ride today. There is a lovely patch of wild herbs along the road heading to the border village. I am in desperate need of coltsfoot." She noticed the firm set of her cousin's mouth. Madeline had known her for far too long and knew when Evelyn was lying.

"I need to go across the border," Evelyn conceded.

Madeline gasped, setting the teacup down with a clatter. "Evelyn, you cannot cross the border. The dangers far outnumber any reward in doing so."

"I have to, Maddy," Evelyn pleaded with her cousin. "I need to investigate something that has come to my attention."

"Send one of the knights. Tell your father," Madeline said, her voice thick with worry. "I beg of you, do not do this."

"But it *is* my responsibility." Evelyn straightened her spine, jutting her chin out slightly. "I cannot trust this to anyone else. I shall return before supper, I promise." There was no dissuading her.

Madeline threw her hands up. "At least take someone with you for protection. Have Sir Alexander accompany you."

Evelyn's head jerked up. "I do not need him to protect me. I am perfectly capable of taking care of myself."

"Please?" Madeline's eyes were large, hazel pools.

She sat torn between placating her cousin's concern for her safety and her thirst for the truth. Evelyn wanted to be sure someone knew to look for her if she did not return. One must always have a contingency plan.

"Very well," Evelyn relented. "I will have him accompany me." She had no intention of following through, but it was better to soothe her cousin's ruffled feathers now, rather than face her ire later.

Madeline's face brightened with relief. Peace restored, the ladies sat together, enjoying a breakfast of porridge, bread, cold meat, and tea.

After the meal, Evelyn progressed to the stables. She saddled Jester, tying some bags to the pommel containing bread, cheese, and a skin of ale. As she led him out into the morning light, a figure stepped away from the building toward her horse, startling them both. A strong hand snatched the reins.

"Going somewhere, my lady?"

Evelyn swore under her breath. *Damn Madeline's persistence.* Sir Alexander moved Jester's head, his handsome face and piercing eyes disorienting her for a moment.

"Aye, Sir Alexander. I fully intend to take advantage of this beautiful day and ride into the village on the other side of the glen." She hoped her nervous hands did not betray her secrets.

He searched her face, his intense gaze threatening not to miss a detail. She swallowed, forcing a smile.

"Allow me to escort you, my lady." He said it with such respect and sincerity Evelyn almost believed he offered out of concern and not obligation. "Lady Madeline asked that I check on you this morning."

Well, there goes that notion. She refused to make a scene in the courtyard. She would have to find a way to lose him along the way. Her mind shifted ideas around, while he appraised her with a raised brow.

"I thank you, Sir Alexander." She graced him with a small curtsey. He released the reins and disappeared into the barn to get his horse. Evelyn pulled herself into the saddle and readjusted her stirrups. A few moments later, he reappeared, leading a beautiful black destrier. With one fluid motion, he was in the saddle astride the powerful beast, motioning for her to lead the way.

Evelyn clicked her tongue, urging Jester into a trot through the main gates and down the path leading to the border town. The heavy footfalls of the warhorse struck a lovely harmony to her palfrey's steps.

"The trees are always lovely and fragrant this time of year," Evelyn commented, admiring the forest as they rode.

He grunted a response.

"Whoa," she said as she brought Jester to a stop and slipped from the saddle. Evelyn entered the trees and dropped to her knees. She ripped sprigs of herbs and stuffed them into the open pouch hanging from her hip belt. Sir Alexander watched from the road. Evelyn returned to her horse, noting the curious look on his face.

"Horehound and garlic," she said, patting the bag on her hip. Both herbs had promising medicinal use, and garlic was always welcomed in the kitchens.

Sir Alexander nodded. As she remounted, his warhorse began walking again. Evelyn stared at his broad back, her frustration with him rising. They approached the village and she formulated a plan to slip away from him.

When they approached the bakers, she implemented it. "Sir Alexander, my father requested I retrieve a new dagger he commissioned from the blacksmith. Would you be so kind as to fetch it for me while I refresh myself here?"

"Of course, my lady." He bowed, heading farther into the village.

Once he was out of view, Evelyn walked Jester behind the baker's cottage. She spun him around, urging him into a run toward the border and the abbey that lay beyond. She glanced over her shoulder. *No one.* She smiled as the wind whipped through her hair, her cloak billowing out behind her. Now she had escaped Sir Alexander's watchful care, it was time to discover who dared to betray her father.

The old abbey lay on Scottish soil, a ruin long forgotten by the English and Scottish alike, cursed by memories best forgotten. Of course, it provided the perfect setting for a clandestine meeting. Gabriel crouched in a tree behind a mound of stones, perfectly positioned to afford him adequate cover. The few men who appeared in the time Gabriel had been waiting seemed unconcerned at the possibility of being discovered or overheard.

He listened as the men told bawdy stories and brawled. None of them stood out as the leader. He sat patiently waiting for the traitorous leader to arrive. A fleeting thought of Lady Evelyn asleep the night before floated over him.

He remembered the softness of her skin. The way his name sounded in her husky murmur as she slept. It had taken all his restraint not to kiss her. Allowing himself to dwell on it for hours while sitting alone in this tree, he wished he had.

A breeze fluttered the leaves shielding him. A faint smell of rosewater and horse sweat caught his attention. *Nay, it cannot be.* Disbelief flooded him as he looked down. Sure enough, shrouded in a dark brown cloak beneath him, Lady Evelyn hid behind the pile of stones.

This woman is the bane of my existence. He swore. It seemed as if he had conjured her with his thoughts. He levered himself out of his hiding spot, dropping to the ground without a sound. Gabriel took careful, quiet steps toward her. Her attention was focused on the men, so he crept up behind her, slipped his hand over her mouth as he wrapped his free arm around her waist, and pulled her to the ground. She struggled until she heard his voice.

"We really have to stop meeting this way, Princess."

Chapter Six

Evelyn sagged against Gabriel's body, relief overwhelming her. He pulled her down until they lay on the damp ground. Her back pressed tight against his chest as his hand stilled over her mouth. Every breath from his lips brushed against her nape, making her heart jump. His body was solid and warm. She moaned against his hand.

"Silence," he whispered. A moment later, the sound of footsteps approached, stopping beyond the pile where she had been hidden.

"No one there," one of the men shouted. "Must have been an animal." The footsteps receded.

Every breath she took smelled of leather, tree bark, and a hint of something male and distinctly him. His body was tense, ready for a fight. Her eyes fluttered closed; her body tingled where they touched. Of course, he would be here. If he was indeed a guardian sent to hover over her like a coddling nursemaid, then he was doing splendidly. How did he know she would be there? He must have been observing from the shadows. It irritated her that she was never able to notice him following her.

Her breath caught when a new thought struck her. *Sir Alexander?* That idea put a distinctive damper on her mood. It made sense. Perhaps she had been overzealous in her dismissal in the village, tipping him off. Sir Alexander was no fool.

"Are you well?" he whispered, his breath brushing her ear. He removed his hand from her mouth.

"I am, Sir Alexander," she replied, her voice laced with bitter sarcasm.

His whole body shook as if he were in the throes of a fit. *What is wrong with him? Is he ill?* Then she heard it, a chuckle. He did his best to keep from making noise, but the sound escaped his lips. He took several deep breaths. His hold on her tightened as his whole body shook with smothered laughter.

"Did something I say amuse you?" she murmured.

"You truly believe I am Sir Alexander?" His velvet whisper tickled her ear. "I told you, my name is Gabriel."

"You could very well be lying to me," she snapped. "How am I to know the truth?"

"I will...quiet, horses approach." He squeezed her against him harder, covering her mouth again.

The thundering of horses hooves snapped Evelyn from her momentary lapse. She was there to uncover a plot and possibly identify a band of traitors. If she were to succeed, it would be wise for her to remember that, even with a strong man pinning her to the forest floor.

"You have arrived, my lord," a deep voice sounded from the group.

"I am. Let us be brief, I have an engagement in the village I can ill afford to miss."

That voice! Vile Richard. She knew he was a seditious charlatan, but a traitor? Evelyn's mind spun. Being a trusted subject of her father, he would be privy to details her father kept even from her. Knowledge that wielded in the right way would ensure power. She listened closely.

"Gentlemen," Richard began, "there is to be an event in the next few weeks that will put us in a position of power. My design is to take control of this barony and then push my way north into Scotland. I require every one of you to aid me in making that happen."

Evelyn's blood roiled at his audacity. *How dare he abuse his position.* She fought against Gabriel's embrace, but he held her fast. The sound of voices approaching caught her attention through the anger-induced haze.

"Let us away, Princess," Gabriel whispered, pulling her up and disappearing into the trees as the group gathered in the ruins of the abbey.

The sunlight faded into the darkening forest. Richard took a stroll around the stone ruins. He met with the mercenaries, relaying their instructions. The plan took hold of the men, their eyes aglitter with the promise of power and wealth. He dismissed them to begin preparations. They did not need to know of their expendable role in this plot.

A dark smile twisted his mouth. Finally, all the years of groveling and bowing, the scrimping and scrounging to maintain his appearance would pay off. Remaining in the baron's confidence would relinquish the finest payoff yet. He walked to the edge of the ruins where they dipped into the forest. Richard climbed the rubble, scanning the shadowed forest.

A wave of unease had swept over him when he addressed the men, as though the trees silently observed. He shrugged. A flickering ray of sunshine reflected off the forest floor at the base of the rocks. He descended, plucking the shiny bauble from the dirt. *A brass button, imprinted with a coat of arms.* Richard clenched the bit of metal in his fist. A sneer curled his lip; he had business to attend, and a naive noble woman needed to be reminded of her proper place.

Evelyn glanced at Gabriel as they rode south, side by side. The setting sun cast a soft glow on his profile. Though most of his face remained obscured under the cowl, she caught a glimpse of a strong chin and mobile lips. It teased her, making her want to see more of his face.

"What made you take up spying, Princess?" His question shook her from her musings.

"Someone had to do it," she mumbled.

"You could have requested my aid."

She gave him a pointed look. "Would you have let me accompany you?" Evelyn took his silence as an affirmation of her assumption. *Nay.*

The sun disappeared into the trees. They pushed their

mounts faster to reach the keep by dark. Evelyn enjoyed the sounds of the forest before Gabriel's voice overlapped them.

"How did you manage to sneak away from Sir Alexander?"

The question struck her. Was he playing a game with her? He could not have known she was with Sir Alexander unless they were one and the same. Right?

"I have been watching you for days, Princess. I know who you talk to, where you go, what you do." His voice held a note of playfulness despite the serious tone. "I know you left the keep with Sir Alexander. Did you knock him off his horse and leave him lying in a ditch along the road?"

"I beg your pardon?" She was affronted. "I did no such thing. To my knowledge, the good knight is hale and hearty."

"You are slippery."

"I used my wits," she huffed and spurred her horse into a trot, gaining distance ahead of him. He followed close behind. Time in his company brought her awareness of him to the surface, nagging at her as though he infected her mind. She wanted to know him. A combination of fear and pride stole the curious questions from her lips, burying them deep inside. The dangerous feelings that could bind her to a man for life scared the devil out of her. "So, since you know so much about my daily activities, I want to know who sent you."

"Pardon?"

"You cannot tell me that your orders do not come from a higher power than my father. Has the king sent you here?" She watched him closely, but he gave nothing away.

"Aye."

"Surely your mission is not merely to protect a poor defenseless woman," she said.

"Nay, my orders are to protect this barony. The border is a volatile place, Princess. Protecting you is only part of my mission."

"Does my father know of your mission?"

"Not yet. 'Tis best if he remains unaware of my existence until we discover who these traitors are, do you agree?"

"Aye." She knew he was right. Silence enveloped them, but

after a few moments, she spoke again. "I am not as helpless as I seem." She caught him glancing at the sword tied to her saddle.

"Do you know how to use that sword?"

"Aye," she said as her hand absently smoothed over the hilt.

He reined his horse to the right, disappearing into the forest. She followed. As they rode deeper into the trees, Evelyn became wary.

"Where are you leading me?" she asked

"Somewhere you can prove yourself," he replied without turning to look at her.

The forest thinned into small, flat clearing. Gabriel dismounted and drew his sword, motioning for her to join him. Evelyn slipped from her saddle and unsheathed her own. Facing him on the field, she nodded.

Gabriel attacked, bringing his blade across to hit her left shoulder. She parried to the left to block him. He switched sides and swiped down toward her right shoulder. Evelyn countered with a parry to the right.

"Is this going to be challenging at some point?" Evelyn smirked.

Gabriel brought his blade across aiming for her left leg, which she blocked, then down to her right. She blocked again.

"Truly? You think me simple?" she asked.

He hesitated, then lunged. When she tilted her sword to parry to the right, he retracted, spinning around her to tap her bottom with the blunt of his blade. She shifted her heated gaze to him. His face was still darkened by the deep hood, but she could sense his amusement.

"That is trickery, a dirty move," she exclaimed, tracking his movements.

"There is no such thing as a fair fight, so fight dirty," he said. "Do you concede?"

"Nay." Evelyn lifted her blade and charged him. He blocked her thrust, parrying to the right, pushing the momentum of the blade around to wrench it from her grasp. Throwing her weight into it, she stomped down on his foot with her heel and twisted it with all her strength.

He dropped back, slipping from her grasp and shaking his foot.

"You learn quickly, Princess."

With a nod, Evelyn stepped forward, her sword up and ready. Gabriel was poised, waiting with his weapon in front of him. She took an arching swipe across his shoulders aiming for his head.

He deftly ducked beneath the blow, taking a step back. She kept her focus on the dark recesses of the hood searching for his eyes. His lips showed a crooked smile. *A challenge.*

She thrust her sword high and aimed for his shoulder. He countered, the clang of the blades echoing as they slid together, meeting at the cross above the hilt. Before she could breathe, one of his hands slipped over hers, holding her steady.

His touch sent a delicious shiver down her spine. She jerked her hand away, wrenching her sword free from his grasp.

"You fight well, Princess." He took a step away from her. "But never underestimate your opponent."

With her free hand, she slipped her dagger from her belt and slung it from her fingertips. It flew past his ear and split the bark as it lodged in the tree behind his head. With a smug tilt of her head, Evelyn tucked her sword back into the sheath on her saddle.

He approached her from the side, her dagger in his hand. She took it, slipping it into the belt on her hip.

"You are well trained. I beg pardon for doubting your abilities." He returned to his horse and led them through the woods.

Evelyn followed him, unsure of his thoughts, knowing her insatiable curiosity would be her ruin. They walked in silence until she noticed the shadow of the keep through the trees. He tied both horses to a branch. Approaching Gabriel, her hand hovered between them for a moment, words failing her.

Her scent wrapped around him like a comforting embrace. He was lost. Nothing could have prepared him for this mission, and nothing could save him from falling under her charm. It was his duty to protect her. But first, he had to protect her from himself.

Her hand lightly touched his shoulder.

"My apologies," she murmured. He glanced at her. Evelyn stared at the walls of the keep through the darkened forest.

"You were right. I should have come to you for help," she began, "but you must understand. I need to do this myself, to prove I am capable."

He searched her face. "I have never seen a woman more capable, although spying is out of your grasp, Princess."

"You may be right. But I need to bring these traitors to justice. If I took this to my father now, he would trust the very man I know to be the leader behind this plot. I need more evidence before I bring it to my father. He has trusted Richard for too long to take my word alone."

"Will you let me help you?" Gabriel asked.

Evelyn's mouth formed a small *o* of surprise. She seemed flustered, and it endeared her to him even more.

"No one has ever asked if I wanted help before. They always assumed I needed it or forced it on me." Her voice wavered as she glanced toward the keep again. "I know the freedoms I enjoy as a woman are unusual. 'Tis one of the things I love most about my father. He gave me the reins."

"And all the other men try to harness you," he finished her thought, finally understanding how much it truly meant to her. He took a step toward her. "Is that why you refuse to marry?"

When she looked at him her eyes were bright with unshed tears, but her smile remained strong as she stepped back away from him. "I am afraid that marriage will put an end to everything I have ever known. Even worse would be a marriage without love."

"So if you loved a man and still held your freedom, would you take a chance?" Gabriel cringed as the ridiculous question left his mouth. He was taken with her and valued her assets.

Would love make the difference? The thought of her with another man sent his thoughts to a dark place deep in his soul. He continued to close the gap between them.

"I am not certain." Evelyn retreated until she bumped into a tree. He pinned her there, his hands on her hips, holding her steady. He knew she was unable see his face, but she searched him. He flinched then reminded himself that his identity was still safely hidden. Perhaps it was wishful thinking, but he wanted her to see him. She placed her palm on his chest. He slid a hand up to cup her chin and caressed the pad of his thumb across her lips.

"Rest assured, Princess, I would never bridle you. A breed like you is rare indeed. Best to let you run free."

Her smile made him sway. Giving into the maddening desire, he captured her lips in a tender kiss, and his heart ripped open. The soft touch lit a fire deep inside of him. He drew her closer, letting their mutual passion weave its magic.

She moaned, sending the desire straight to his loins. Her arms snaked their way around his torso. When she opened her mouth and darted her tongue across his lips, he deepened the kiss. Their tongues danced as his hands roamed her back. She clutched at him like she was starving and he was the first meal she had seen in days.

Gabriel's desire rose to a boiling point. He had to stop this madness before it was beyond control. Saints, he hated the thought of letting her go. He wanted to take her, to make her his forever. She tasted like heaven, like mint and fresh highland air. Intoxicating. He gently pushed her away. His hands firm on her shoulders as he leaned his forehead against hers.

"Evelyn." He whispered her name like a prayer. She sighed, dropping her hands to her sides.

"You should go. They will be concerned for your well-being," he said, his heart pounding in his chest. "I will be here if you need me."

She nodded and returned to her horse, pulling herself into the saddle.

"Princess," he called to her. She turned to glance at him.

"You said Sir Richard was the man leading this?"

"Aye."

"Did you recognize any of the other men?" His curiosity bloomed.

"I did not see any of the men nor recognize any of their voices."

"You are positive it their leader was Sir Richard though?"

Her gaze narrowed when she answered, "I swear my life on it."

He nodded as she favored him with a farewell smile and disappeared into the keep. Gabriel leaned against the large tree. He stared at the keep, now shrouded in darkness, and wondered what the hell he had gotten himself into this time.

Chapter Seven

Evelyn arrived in time to join the household for the evening meal. The food tasted delicious. Evelyn had neglected her growling stomach all day. While she ate, Madeline kept her entertained, laughing and sharing witty tales. The tingle of a blush spread across her cheeks, remembering Gabriel's kiss. It forever branded her as well as kept her distracted for he still lingered in the shadows of her mind. Evelyn sighed.

"Evelyn, are you well?" her father asked.

She offered him a smile. "Aye, Father. Just tired from my visit to the village. I believe I shall retire." She stood, leaning down to kiss her father's grizzled cheek. His smile could not undo the concern on his face. She turned to leave the great hall, anxious to be away.

Evelyn climbed the stairs to her chamber. Her mind was cloudy, drunk on the memory of Gabriel's arms, his lips. She shook the romantic musings from her head. *It was only a kiss.* His fervent response proved he had a weakness for her.

"How fare you, my lady?" Sir Richard's voice echoed behind her. "I see you went riding this day. May I ask where your adventure led you?" Some might consider him handsome, his charm wooing many a woman. His stare was dark under his arched brow, and his words laced with thinly veiled contempt.

"I...uh, to the village," she stammered, flustered by his menacing presence. Evelyn fought to contain her reaction. She avoided him whenever she could, fearing he may push the boundary of propriety. "I spent the day in the village with Sir Alexander."

"Is that so?" His eyes gleamed. "Why do I not believe you?" He leaned close. His hand brushed against hers, slipping an object in her palm. Richard whispered in her ear, "I know you were at the abbey."

She jerked away from his wine-sweetened breath, shooting

him a look of contempt. Curiosity overwhelmed her as she glanced down at her palm.

"Look familiar? It should. That is your family crest on the button, is it not?"

Evelyn stared speechless at the brass button in her hand. She closed her fist, biting her tongue to halt an ill-considered response. *He has me trapped.*

"You can always join me." His voice snaked over her, making her skin crawl. Richard placed his hand on her hip and trailed his palm up over her curves to cup her breast. She pulled away from him and spit in his face.

"Bitch!" He hissed, grabbing a fistful of her hair and snapping her head back.

Then her head fell free, the stench of Sir Richard's breath vanishing. The movement sent her reeling, and she braced her hand against the wall to steady herself. Sir Alexander had her assailant by the collar and turned, tossing Sir Richard down the staircase as a string of profanities streamed from his vulgar lips. Her rescuer stood before her, his stance pulsing with tightly leashed fury.

"Did he hurt you, my lady?" Sir Alexander asked. "Would you like me to fetch your father?"

"Nay, I thank you." She assured him, her voice trembling. "I am quite well."

"He accosted you," he spoke calmly, but she saw the rage boiling inside of him.

"I pray you, Sir Alexander," she begged. "Do not tell anyone."

Alexander looked at her, his expression a mix of fury and control. Her hand flew to her hair, smoothing it back into her braid. Her face burned with embarrassment and injured pride. She wrapped her arms around herself furious Richard would dare lay a hand on her in her father's house. Evelyn had been fortunate Sir Alexander happened by at that moment.

"Are you positive?" His words were gentle, but she could hear the anger weaving its tendrils into his voice. "Such behavior should not be tolerated, my lady."

She nodded her head, her gaze meeting his. "Aye, Sir Alexander. He will not escape punishment." He nodded at her determination.

Alexander pursed his lips and obviously decided not to pursue the subject further. Evelyn had good reasons for not sounding the alarm even though Richard deserved to be tossed in the dungeon. Being a traitor was a higher offense than assaulting the baron's daughter. She would tell her father, when the time was right. She needed Sir Richard to believe himself above the law, safe from suspicion. If she played her hand now, it would compromise her investigation into this brewing plot. Richard believed all women to be weak and insignificant. Evelyn would play into his delusion, and in the end he would pay for all his sins.

"Your actions this afternoon were unwise," he chastised. "I was only doing my duty to protect you." His comment broke Evelyn from her thoughts.

"Aye, and I do humbly thank you. Something important arose and I could not wait on your return from the blacksmith." She inspected a frayed hem as she smoothed her skirt.

"You must realize by now there are those who wish to do you harm." His voice softened, almost endearing. "You have an important role in this barony and must take precautions to protect yourself."

"Gra'mercy, Sir Alexander. Your concern is touching." She looked at him, a smile playing on her lips.

He nodded. "Pray pardon me, my lady, I am late for my post." Alexander retreated into the night air.

Richard brooded next to the fire, nursing a mug of ale. He had not counted on Sir Alexander intervening on the lady's behalf. He scoffed. That woman proved to be more trouble than she was worth. His offer for her hand would have solved two problems at once. If marrying Lady Evelyn was no longer an option, he still had some tricks up his sleeve. He smiled against the rim, allowing the heady ale to splash against his lips.

"Drowning your bruised ego?"

Glancing to the right, he spotted Sir Alexander in the shadows. The knight stepped closer, a heavy crease between his brows and his arms locked across his chest. *Self-righteous prick.*

"Away with you, bothersome fly." Richard waved his hand, dismissing the knight.

"I should call you out." Sir Alexander scowled.

Richard glanced over his drink, nonplussed by the knight's half-assed challenge.

"That would be unwise for I have the ear of the baron." He locked gazes with Sir Alexander. "And you have nothing."

"Believe what you will, knave. But know this. If you lay your hands on Lady Evelyn again, I will remove them from your wrists myself." With those words, Sir Alexander departed, leaving Richard alone with his thoughts once again.

He tossed the half empty mug into the fire and returned to his room, slamming the door behind him.

"Bastard!" Richard roared into the empty cavern of his chamber. "Yet another braying hound sniffing around the baron's daughter." Richard threw himself into the chair in front of the fire. He dug the tip of his dagger in the armrest, snapping his wrist, flinging bits of wood into the air. Disgusted, he tossed the knife to the floor.

The room boasted items that belied the wealth of the occupant. The velvet draperies, the goose down bed, and the metallic shimmer of a mirror in the corner of the room presented the illusion of wealth. The truth was far less appealing. The fancy trappings and private room were gifts of gratitude from the baron and the king for years of faithful service. Long ago, the king made a promise to elevate Richard from knight to baron. Instead, His Majesty foisted him on an obscure baron tucked next to the border. He had spent years garnering the baron's trust and favor.

The Baron of Rayne was unaware of the delightful events Richard planned in conjunction with the spring tournament. He would make himself a hero and in return accept the barony as gratitude for service to the crown. The only question that remained was how the daughter fit into his scheme.

"That girl is about to get a rude introduction to the reality of her situation," he glowered staring into the fire, his fingers steepled in thought. "Next time I catch her poking around where she does not belong, I will take the steps necessary to ensure her silence."

Gabriel hid in the woods outside the postern gate. His perch halfway up an accommodating tree gave him an unobstructed view into the garden while allowing him to blend into the darkness. He stared over the stone wall, his thoughts interrupted by a vision of Lady Evelyn, breathless from his kiss.

"Lover boy, climb down from your perch," a harsh growl echoed from the base of the tree. Gabriel disentangled himself from the tree branches, dropping to the ground on silent feet.

"Good eve, Alexander. How are things inside the keep?"

Alexander leaned against the tree. "I caught Sir Richard accosting Lady Evelyn." He put a hand up. "Before you get worked into frenzy, I took measures to ensure her safety."

"Are you sure?" he asked, the fury seeping into his voice. Every muscle in Gabriel's body tensed as he flexed his hand into a fist. He had not been there. He reminded himself Alexander protected her inside the keep. "Of course you are or you would not have left her alone."

"I sent Richard running with his tail tucked between his legs," Alexander said with confidence.

"Richard attacked her?" Gabriel asked through clenched teeth. "Did you inform the baron?"

"I would have, but Lady Evelyn swore me to secrecy."

"He was the man orchestrating the rendezvous at the abbey." Gabriel wondered if Richard somehow knew of her...their presence.

"I have never seen Richard treat Lady Evelyn in such a manner before. Why would he corner her tonight?"

"Because she slipped away from you and appeared below my tree as I waited at the abbey. But how Richard knew she had been there confounds me."

"Were you able to identify any of the men at the abbey?" Alexander asked.

Gabriel opened his mouth to answer, when an impulsive and selfish idea struck him.

"I need to get inside the keep, Alexander."

"We both know why you want to be in the keep, Gabe. I know you fancy Lady Evelyn; you make no secret of that. You moon over her like a lovesick calf, and 'tis distracting you from your real mission." Alexander gave him a pointed look.

"I know," he replied. "But if I can get inside, I can identify the other men from the abbey. I have a feeling Richard is not the only one in the keep involved in this plot."

"If I let you inside, can I be certain that you will maintain my good name?" Alexander's expression was one of complete seriousness. "I need you to promise to be on your best behavior."

"Aye, mother," Gabriel teased. *Typical Alexander.*

"You know how important it is to maintain the charade," Alexander continued, as he removed his vest and sword.

Gabriel pulled the hood from his head and tossed it to Alexander. "Wear it well, dear brother."

"Only if you do my name justice."

As they traded garments, the moonlight shifted through the trees, illuminating the pair as they faced each other tugging their weapons into place. Gabriel smiled at his twin. *This is always the fun part.*

Evelyn lay in her bed entranced by the dancing shadows on the wall. Her father always believed she had a knack for finding trouble. Now it seemed it had found her. She curled up, burying her head beneath the covers.

This day did not go at all as she had planned. *Am I doomed to be shadowed by Gabriel for eternity?* She would have gotten more information at the abbey had he not shown up. Evelyn considered the situation again. Had it not been for his intervention she would have been discovered. She sat up and pounded a fist into her pillow. When it had been satisfactorily fluffed, Evelyn slammed her head down again.

What really bothered her about Gabriel was his innate ability to unsettle her composure. She took pride in being able to control her emotions, especially when it came to men. What made him so different? His face was always hidden by that damned cowl. He could be hideous for all she knew.

Evelyn kicked the covers in frustration, then pulled them back over her head. She hated that she could do nothing without her thoughts turning to him. She wanted him to touch her, whisper to her, kiss her. The memory of his kiss faded into an image of Richard groping her.

A tremor racked her body as she remembered Richard's hands on her. The sweet, sickly stench of his breath made her physically ill. *The cur!* When Alexander stopped him, she nearly expired from relief and mortification. One could only imagine what Richard would have done had Sir Alexander not intervened. Her stomach roiled at the thought.

Evelyn wanted to tell her father. Nothing would have given her more pleasure than to see him punished for what he did, but her silence was part of a broader plan. She needed Richard to believe himself safe and above the consequences of his actions. Her certainty that he led the rebels gave her reason to wait for the opportune moment to expose him.

She heaved a sighed. After today, Evelyn trusted Gabriel with her safety. When they kissed, she came close to trusting him with her heart. *If only he would trust me with his identity.*

Memory of his smell, his touch, his taste, soothed her. It also created another dilemma. The more time she spent in his company, the closer she came to falling in love with the mysterious Gabriel. He ignited a desire for companionship she never thought she would be fortunate enough to find. Never had she wanted a man. It terrified her, thrilled her. *How can I choose between my freedom or him?*

She groaned as she punched the pillow, fluffing it again. As sleep struggled to claim her, she indulged in the fantasy of a life with Gabriel. Evelyn drifted off with a smile on her lips.

Chapter Eight

"Wake up, Evelyn."

A surly voice cut through Evelyn's wonderful dream of Gabriel tugging the cowl back away from his face...

"Evelyn!"

...then nothing. The bright rays of sunlight stung her vision. Madeline stood over her bed, arms crossed, tapping her foot impatiently.

"Evelyn, 'tis past midday. Perhaps you could summon a reason to get out of bed?" Madeline's frown echoed her disappointment.

"Oh Madeline, I forgot about our morning tea," she groaned.

"'Twas the first day fine enough for us to break our fast in the garden," Madeline pouted. "And you missed it!"

"I beg your pardon, Maddy, truly. I found it difficult to sleep." Evelyn rose from the bed. "Would you help me?" she asked, gesturing to her clothes.

"Must not have been too difficult," Madeline scoffed. "You were sleeping like a lamb when I came in earlier. I tried to wake you, but you kept mumbling something about a shadow. And who is Gabriel?"

"I have not the faintest idea what you mean, Madeline." She pushed the questions aside as she brushed and plaited her hair.

Madeline harrumphed. *Now what has put her in such a foul mood?* Evelyn glanced at her cousin. Normally Madeline was never surly and certainly never rude.

"Who upset your teapot this morning?" Evelyn asked. She put on a working gown and tied the laces. "And do not tell me it was my absence that put you in such a state. Has one of your admirers crossed you?"

"Och, Evey," Madeline flopped onto the bed. "I did not want to say anything. I know you dislike him."

Evelyn cocked her head, intrigued. *Who could...?* Then she pieced it together. "Are you referring to Sir Alexander?"

"Aye." She chewed her lower lip. "I do not know if he admires me. We rarely speak, but sometimes I catch him staring at me."

Evelyn smiled, relieved that her cousin finally noticed the knight's interest. "So what is the problem? Go flirt, tease him, and leave him with no doubt of your affections."

"I greeted him this morning. He looked at me as though he had never seen me before this day. And he not looked in my direction, not once all day."

"Hmmm..." Evelyn mused, tapping her chin. "I am sure all is well. Give him time. Perhaps your beauty causes him to forget himself?"

A giggle escaped Madeline's lips. "I doubt that entirely. Do you really think he will come around?"

"Absolutely," Evelyn assured her. "Now, come. Since I missed tea in the garden, shall we spy on the guards through the rose arbor? Perhaps we shall catch a glimpse of a certain knight."

Madeline waved her hand. "I am sure he is out with the baron, taking stock of the barony and meeting with the farmers. Or possibly sparring in the courtyard." The duo headed down the staircase.

"I believe you find reasons to pass the knight's quarters while they practice, my dear cousin."

Madeline grinned at Evelyn. "Perhaps."

Evelyn and Madeline stepped into the blossoming oasis tucked in the back of the keep, giggling like children as they wandered toward their favorite bench.

"I know what we need," Evelyn declared, feeling exceptionally naughty. "Some of father's scotch. I shall return." She slipped from the gardens and into the kitchen, making her way to her father's presence chamber. Her father was out riding, meeting with the farmers near the village. He made it clear she should keep away from his whisky, but she enjoyed sneaking it once in a while. It always emboldened her. Right now, she and Madeline needed a little pick-me-up.

"Good day, my lady," a masculine voice made her jump as she entered the kitchen. She turned.

"Good morrow, Sir Alexander," she smiled. He looked as he did last night. Tall, handsome, confident, but there was laughter dancing in his blue eyes. *How odd.*

"Now that I have seen you, I can say with all honesty that my day will not get any better. So I bid you good eve." He laughed in jest.

Evelyn stood with her mouth hanging open, stunned. *Sir Alexander laughing and teasing me with lighthearted humor.* Madeline was correct in assuming all was not well with Sir Alexander.

"Madeline and I are having a picnic in the gardens, would you care to join us for some scots whisky?" she offered.

"I dare say that sounds like an intriguing proposal." His smile made her heart stop. "Alas, I cannot join you. I must attend some business. Fare you well, my lady." And with a bow, he left her.

Evelyn stared after him, her jaw askew. *Had he taken a hit to the head last evening?* That could be the only explanation for Sir Alexander's miraculous transformation.

Madeline held a tendre for Sir Alexander. Up until this morning, she would have sworn on the Holy Word he held one for Madeline as well. *Best keep my distance from him.* Evelyn snatched the whisky from the cabinet under her father's desk and rejoined her cousin in the garden.

The sun shone down on Gabriel's face as he strolled through the courtyard. He took a deep breath. The relief to be out from under the cowl relaxed him. Since he spent most of his time wearing it, this was truly a rare treat. Alexander always walked in the light while Gabriel remained hidden in the shadows. But the real blessing was, as identical twins, they could easily trade places.

He stood face to face with Evelyn. Of course, she had no

idea she was speaking with Gabriel and not Alexander. The scoundrel in him loved the irony. He had to keep with his brother's mannerisms and routine, but he could not pass up a chance to tease her. Lady Evelyn made him want a lot of things he never thought he could have, most of all a woman who challenged him. His heart ached at the thought, so he pushed the dreams away. He had a job to do.

Gabriel joined the other knights training in the inner bailey. Alexander and Gabriel had trained together for years, perfecting their fighting style so it was identical. When they fought side by side, it transformed into a dance, carefully choreographed in tandem. They had traded places in the past, so it became easy to fall into his brother's role. Alexander was so rigid and predictable. Gabriel, the younger twin by two minutes, was not.

He took his shirt off and leaned against the wall, awaiting the end of the current bout. Gabriel watched the men fight.

He replayed the conversation with Evelyn from just moments ago, remembering he must remain in character with his brother lest she realize something was amiss. It proved difficult for him stay in Alexander's character when she was near. He wanted to kiss her again, show her who he truly was without the shadow of his mission hovering over them. Shaking the thoughts, he forced himself to pay attention to the mission at hand and not the sable haired vixen who shook his convictions.

The beautiful blue skies persisted into the late afternoon. Evelyn walked in the woods outside the gate to collect herbs for her medicine box. It occupied her time and gave her an excuse to leave the keep. The stone walls did wonders for warding off uninvited guests, but it felt like a prison when one remained inside too long.

She slipped through the postern gate with a basket under her arm. Evelyn dawdled as she walked through the forest. In the back of her mind, she formulated a plan to catch Sir Richard and his conspirators. The snake had found her out. Though she refused to acknowledge being at the abbey, his expression spoke volumes. *Thank heavens for Sir Alexander.*

Evelyn knelt in the damp meadow by the stream, collecting some marsh mallow and mint. She put the items in her basket and rose. The blue skies and waning sunlight told her a fair night lay ahead. She wandered through the woods near the stream to collect some willow twigs. Perhaps Gabriel would come to her. She shook her head at the ridiculous notion. Yet it lingered like an echo in her heart.

A lone male figure stood on the edge of the woods, leaning on a sturdy trunk, his gaze following her. He wore no cowl. Her heart sank. She walked, keeping her gaze focused on him.

"No escort again, my lady?" Sir Alexander asked.

Of course, he would come looking for me.

"Good day, Sir Alexander." She flashed a hesitant smile. "I stepped outside the gates to pick some herbs. Surely that does not require an escort."

"May I accompany you?" Alexander's mahogany hair was tousled and damp. His bright eyes took in her every movement.

"I suppose," she replied, hesitant. "You have a habit of appearing at odd moments, Sir Alexander."

They walked side by side through the forest.

"Mayhap we are attuned to each other," he said.

"Or perhaps you are following me," she countered, casting him a wary look. *Attuned to each other?* Sir Alexander had never shown this much interest in her before. She studied his face. His lips quirked in a playful grin.

"'Tis my duty to ensure your safety, my lady," he swore. "'Tis a small keep making it feasible I happen upon you by chance every time."

"For certain." She watched him with a blend of curiosity and skepticism. "You suddenly enjoy lively conversation with me. That is quite a surprise, for a few days ago I could have sworn you abhorred the very thought of exchanging words with me."

Evelyn turned when she noted Sir Alexander had stopped

walking. His lips were pursed in thought. After a tense moment, he relaxed and fell into step beside her once again.

"One would think after last evening the nature of our relationship has changed. Has it not?" he asked.

"I suppose rescuing a lady from unwanted attentions would make you an ally, if not a friend," Evelyn replied. A small flare of heat blossomed across her cheeks at the strange direction of the conversation.

"Are you saying we are friends now, my lady?"

"You came to my aid and for that I thank you," she replied. "Friendship, I find, takes time to develop."

"I see." He snatched a handful of leaves from a bush as they passed by. He let them glide through his fingertips and fall to the ground.

"You seem different this day," she commented. "I suppose the events of last eve did forge a kind of bond between us."

"Aye, it did. We have arrived, my lady," he bowed, allowing her to pass through the gates ahead of him. When he joined her side, he took her hand in his and brushed a lingering kiss on her knuckles. "I shall see you anon." He turned and disappeared into the great hall without a backward glance.

Evelyn stood, stunned, in the middle of the bailey. *What in God's name has gotten into Sir Alexander?*

Chapter Nine

The waning moon and torchlight illuminated the grounds as Gabriel resumed his duty guarding the postern gate. He spent most of the day milling around inside the keep, listening and observing. None of them triggered any resemblance to the men at the abbey. He walked outside the barbican, staring into the darkened forest.

"Keeping vigilant watch are you?" came a voice from the shadows to his left.

Gabriel approached the source of the voice. "Good to see you too, brother mine."

Alexander leaned against the stone wall. "Have you identified anyone yet?"

"Nay," Gabriel replied. "None of them look or sound familiar. I will continue my search on the morrow." He paused and looked at his brother. "You have not come to replace me, have you?"

"Would I have any cause to do that?" Alexander stood, unflinching. "I saw you with Lady Evelyn this afternoon. You talk too much."

"You are not an easy person to imitate. Your conversational skills are just below a mute," he teased. "Do you want me not to speak the entire time I am you?"

"Aye," Alexander said, "but I realize that for you that is an impossibility. Could you at least shelve your infatuation for the moment?"

Gabriel took a deep breath. "You are right," he said. "I let my attraction to her affect the mission. I promise to focus on what needs to be done."

"My thanks," Alexander stepped up to him and placed his hands on Gabriel's shoulders. "I must go. Meet me here at week's end. We can switch back then."

Gabriel watched as his brother disappeared into the night.

His heart sank a little as he returned to his post. *So much for being close to her.*

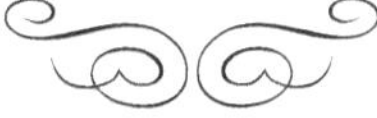

Over the next three days, Evelyn kept to the stillroom and gardens. Sir Richard had been hovering around her father since the incident. With her father so preoccupied, Evelyn only spoke to him at the evening meals. So she enlisted the help of her cousin in preparing some herbal tinctures and salves to keep her occupied. She gathered the herbs she required and busied herself.

In keeping occupied with a task, Evelyn found it easier to push thoughts of Gabriel from her mind. The tournament also rapidly approached, although a majority of the work for its preparation had already been delegated. She set the most recent ointment to cool then wandered into the garden to indulge in the spring air.

As she exited the stillroom, Evelyn caught a glimpse of Sir Alexander as he disappeared into the courtyard. Ever since their conversation in the forest, he was always in her sight but never able to engage in conversation. Perhaps it was for the best; she was beginning to enjoy his company and feared it would only upset Madeline. The poor dear was beside herself, fearing Sir Alexander had quite lost interest in her. *Aye, this is to be the only solution.*

Evelyn walked through the garden, under the arbor, then through the postern gate. The sun was setting, and shadows romped through the forest. She sat down on a stump, staring off into the twilight when she heard his approach.

"I thought you had abandoned me completely." She chuckled. The shadow guardian stood silent in front of her. "No witty rejoinder?"

He shook his head. The black cowl shielded his face as usual.

She stood and sashayed over to him, placing her hand on his chest. "I know this is unlike me...but I have missed your company." She looked at him, hopeful.

"Return to the keep," he murmured, his voice smooth and stern.

Evelyn dropped her hand in disappointment. After their last encounter, she anticipated a bit of flirtation. Something had changed. Perhaps he had seen her with Sir Alexander and believed she entertained flirtations from another man.

"Are you angry with me?" The words slipped from her lips before she could stop them. *What should I care what he thought?* Somewhere deep inside, his cold tone ripped at her heart.

"You need to stay inside the keep, unless you are properly escorted." His normally velvet voice held an icy edge.

She stared at him, her jaw gaping. How could he treat her in such a way after their last meeting, after such a kiss? Tears stung her eyes. She dashed them away with her hands, refusing to let him see her cry.

He said nothing, but when she made no move to leave, he crossed his arms.

She backed away. "I shall return." Evelyn ran to the keep as fast as she could, without so much as a backward glance. As Evelyn entered the gate, she met Madeline leaving the kitchen.

"How fare you, Evelyn?" Madeline called out as she passed by.

"I am well," she tossed over her shoulder, shielding her tear-streaked face behind her hand.

Evelyn climbed the staircase leading to her chamber. Rounding the corner, she collided with Sir Alexander and collapsed as his strong hands gripped her arms.

"Lady Evelyn, are you well?" His blue eyes searched her face. His strength seeped into her, warming deep into her soul. He smelled like rain and the faint hint of leather. She wet her lips, forcing herself to think. This was Alexander. *Madeline...I cannot...*

"I am well. Please let me pass." She hiccuped, grappling for a reserve of strength.

"Nay. You are weeping. Has Richard harmed you again? I will hunt him down and..." Evelyn raised a hand, silencing his words.

"It was not Richard. It..." She stopped, realizing she could not say it without revealing Gabriel's secret.

"It, what?" He pushed.

"Let me pass, I beg you." Sir Alexander's strong embrace intensified her frustration. Fresh tears burst from her before she could stop them.

He cradled her against his chest as his hands caressed her back in comforting circles. Afraid of what she might see, Evelyn peeked up at him. His handsome face, framed by his deep brown locks, hovered above her, his tempting mouth a heartbeat from hers. She reached her hand up to cup his cheek. His eyes closed as his hands stilled. Tilting her head and raising herself up, she sealed his lips with hers. He pulled her into his arms, and she sighed against his mouth when he kissed her in return.

"I have missed you, Princess," he whispered in a velvet voice.

Chapter Ten

Evelyn pulled away from him, their breaths coming in rapid puffs. Her eyes were hazed with desire but well aware of his blunder.

"What did you just call me?"

"Um..."

"You *are* the shadow guardian!" She beat his chest with her fists. "How dare you treat me thus, as a child who has done wrong! Why did you lie to me? Why?"

He grabbed her flailing fists. "Evelyn, stop. I am the shadow guardian."

"Let me go," she screamed, jerking from his grip. "What is your name, your real name?" She took a few steps back.

"My name is Gabriel," he admitted but held back, unsure of how he would dig himself out of his accidental slip-of-the-tongue.

Gabriel looked down into her tear-streaked face, searching her luminous green eyes. He could not tell her everything. No matter how much he wanted to soothe her conscience, to explain himself. He needed to talk to Alexander first.

"Forsooth." She threw her hands up. "You will tell me nothing?"

"Aye, right now this is all I can offer." He sighed. "But I promise you, I will reveal everything to you on the morrow." He captured her hand and placed it over heart. "I swear it."

"I do not believe you." She tore her hand from his. "I do not know what to believe." She pushed past him and disappeared into her chamber, slamming the door behind her.

"What have I done?" Gabriel leaned his forehead on the wall. The stone cooled the heat raging in his face. Pushing off the wall, he strode down the stairs, out the postern gate, and into the forest.

Evelyn leaned against her door as she buried her face in her hands. A sob escaped her lips, then another. Before she realized it, her hands were soaked with tears. She grabbed her sword and swung it with all her strength at an unoffending bedpost. Her blows rained down on the post, bits of wood splintering in all directions. Every strike sent vibrations up her arms.

"God's blood, teeth, and bones!" She swore as the sword collided with the wood again. It bit deep into the solid oak. Profanities poured from her lips as she assaulted the inanimate object. Evelyn, blinded by her rage, assaulted the post until she could stand no more.

She collapsed on the floor, her body weary and her head throbbing. The tears dried as the unspoken words pierced her chest. Evelyn had betrayed her cousin and herself. Sir Alexander, Gabriel, whoever he said he was, must think her a common strumpet. Nothing made sense.

Conflict raged a battle in Evelyn's mind. She sighed, her heart breaking.

The sword slipped from her hands. She climbed into her bed and pulled the blankets over her head. As exhaustion claimed her body, sleep settled over her in an attempt to rest her weary soul.

Gabriel stepped over fallen branches and wove between the trees. The call of the nighttime animals echoed around him. Determined to right what he had done wrong, he set his jaw before stopping at the base of a large oak tree.

"Alexander, come down, we need to talk."

"What happened, Gabe?" His brother asked as he emerged from behind the tree.

Momentarily surprised by the location of Alexander's

appearance, he cleared his throat. "I fear there has been a complication." Gabriel leaned against the tree.

"What did you do?"

"Ah, see there, what makes you believe I did anything?" He glowered at his brother.

"You are impulsive by nature, and it never fails to catch up to you," Alexander replied. "What happened?"

"Lady Evelyn knows I am the shadow guardian."

Alexander cursed under his breath.

"She also believes that the shadow guardian and Sir Alexander are one and the same," he finished before his brother could comment.

Gabriel could imagine the look of disbelief on Alexander's face. He had received that look from his brother before, and it always made him feel like a naughty child.

"Explain," Alexander said. His vocal emphasis on the word highlighted his frustration.

"Lady Evelyn was distraught," he began. "I tried to comfort her, and then she kissed me. I called her princess. She recognized it from when I use that term as the shadow guardian."

"I see," Alexander sounded unconvinced, "and what did you tell her?"

"I promised to tell her everything on the morrow." Gabriel glanced away. "I needed to talk to you before I said another word." He refocused his attention back on his brother. "I will not lie to her again."

"It was a wise decision for you to remain silent until we could speak," Alexander replied. "I advised you to distance yourself."

"I tried," he sighed, "but seeing her upset was more than I could bear. Once she recognized me as the shadow guardian, she unleashed her ire on me, blaming me for her tears."

Alexander swore again. "I caught her outside the gate at dusk and told her to go inside."

Evelyn thought it had been him. When he last saw her as the guardian, they shared a lover's embrace. She would have expected a warmer greeting than Alexander provided. But his brother knew nothing of the kiss or his terrible lack of self-control. The irony that her tears were ultimately his fault hit him like a fist to the gut. He needed to set this right.

"We have to tell her, Alexander," Gabriel stated. "We need her help in outing Sir Richard and his band of brigands. She deserves to know the truth."

"You trust her?"

"I do."

"You are not just saying that because you are smitten with her?" His brother arched a brow.

"Aye, 'tis no secret that I care for her. But I firmly believe she could be an asset."

"Very well, Gabriel. On the morrow, bring her to the clearing just over the ridge. We can tell her together. I doubt she will believe you any other way."

"I shall see you anon, brother. Do not fall from your perch." Gabriel turned, following the path, his step a little lighter.

When Evelyn woke the next morning, her body ached from her fight with the bedpost. She disentangled herself from the blankets, sluggish and tired. She chose a simple dark green gown and dressed, then descended to the solar. A little nourishment followed by a walk in the morning sun would lift her spirits.

Madeline glanced up as she entered the solar.

"Good morrow, Evelyn. How fair you?" Her cousin returned to the embroidery in her lap.

"Good day," she hedged, unable to face her friend after what transpired the prior evening. She winced. *Why must everything be so complicated?*

"Taking a walk in the garden?" Madeline asked as Evelyn grabbed several pastries from the breakfast tray.

"Aye."

"Can you bring me back a handful of lavender?" Madeline called as Evelyn walked to the door.

"Of course," she replied, shame dragging behind her.

Evelyn stepped into the garden with the morning sun shining bright and warm on her face. She smiled at the sight of colorful blossoms popping up around her. This place and riding were her only true havens. Perhaps a long ride with Jester would clear the fog from her head.

Madeline's request for lavender fell to the wayside as Evelyn bustled to the stables. As she passed under the rose arbor, she stopped. Sir Alexander, who claimed his real name was Gabriel, stood before her. Her skin warmed recounting his touch, his kiss. She was determined to be angry with him. In truth, she was angry with herself.

"Good morrow." He greeted, proffering his arm.

"Sir Alexander," she replied coolly as she snaked her arm through his. Evelyn was still upset with him, but she did not want to make a scene by refusing a social custom. His arm, strong against her own, caused her desire to rush to the surface.

"I was about to go for a ride. Would you care to join me?"

"Aye," she said. "I was already heading to the stables myself."

Evelyn saw him glance at her. His smile touched his eyes, making them sparkle in the morning light. When they were well away from the stone walls, she planned on demanding some answers from the knight.

Chapter Eleven

Evelyn reveled in the earthy scents as they rode through the woods. The silence stretched taut between them. Gabriel led her over the ridge and into a beautiful clearing. They pulled their horses to a halt beside a fallen tree and dismounted, tying the reins off.

"You owe me an explanation," she said as she turned to face him. His blue eyes were even brighter today. She inhaled, steeling herself against the attraction that consumed her.

"Aye."

"Who are you?" she asked, placing several feet between them. "The truth this time." She crossed her arms. A flutter of movement just beyond Gabriel's head caught her attention. A figure, shroud in black and wearing a cowl, stepped from the tree line into the clearing behind Gabriel.

Evelyn slipped the dagger from her belt. "You tricked me!" The man approached them. *What have I gotten myself into?* She had been a fool to trust him. First, she betrayed her best friend and now herself by falling into the enemy's hands. Gabriel turned and took a step toward her. "Deciever! Do not move."

She drew the knife up, the tip glinting in the morning sun. "Have you decided to kidnap me? Kill me? Try it." She charged at the man in black, a guttural cry ripping from her lips. Gabriel snatched her by the waist with one arm as his other hand twisted the knife from her grasp.

"We bear you no ill intent, Evelyn," he said as she struggled against his powerful hold. "If you promise not to gut us, I will explain."

She stilled in his arms, not because she trusted him, but because there were two of them. Without her sword, she was outmatched.

"Why does he wear the garb of the shadow guardian? You told me you were the shadow guardian?" The fear lingered in the back of her mind, and confusion clouded her heart.

Gabriel's hold loosened a fraction; his steady voice caressed her ear. "I am the shadow guardian."

"Then who is that? A figment of my imagination?"

"He is my brother," he replied.

"My father told me your brother was dead. Why are you hiding him?" Evelyn asked in confusion.

"We work better as a team when only one of us is exposed," Gabriel explained. "The king sent us here, as a team, to maintain the peace. We are here as a precaution. Not to start a war, but possibly prevent one."

Evelyn's mind absorbed his words, but she struggled to fathom why he hid his brother. Her father would accept both the men in his court if they were truly here to help and protect the borderlands.

"Why hide one?"

The shadow guardian stepped closer, his voice low. "Sometimes 'tis important strategically to be able to confound and outmaneuver your enemy within the shadows."

She searched him, her jaw thrust forward. His face was obscured by the cowl. Evelyn remained unconvinced.

The hooded man reached up and slipped the cowl back. Evelyn's eyes widened in disbelief.

"You are *twins?*" she screamed, tearing herself from Gabriel's grasp. She backed away from both men. Her dagger pointed at them in accusation.

The man in black crossed the gap, stopping next to the knight she had accompanied to the glen. They both faced her. Her gaze flickered between them. She needed a moment to swallow this revelation, to allow her mind to process what she saw.

"Aye, identical twins," Gabriel spoke softly. "This is my brother Alexander."

Evelyn stared at the brothers in shock. They were identical, from their thick wavy mahogany hair to their stature, from eye color to height. She stood comparing them, studying one then the other, searching for a discrepancy, something to tell them apart.

She took a hesitant step closer, her gaze focused on their faces. Gabriel and Alexander had one distinct difference. Gabriel's blue eyes held a laughing shimmer of light, revealing his playful nature. Alexander's were colder, more serious. The bright blue of a cloudless summer sky compared to the icy hue that descends just before a winter storm.

Placing a hand on her hip, she waited for their explanation.

Alexander and Gabriel shared a look. Nodding at his brother, Gabriel turned to Evelyn. "When we arrived, Alexander took the position inside the keep and I as the shadow guardian."

She nodded for him to continue, her mind replaying the last fortnight.

"When I escorted you home after the abbey, we switched places. It was to be for a few days, so I could identify the men at the abbey." He continued, "As you may have gathered by now, my brother and I may look alike, but our personalities are vastly different."

"Aye." She crossed her arms, still maintaining a wary watch on the men. A wave of relief enveloped Evelyn. "So then...It was not..." she mumbled, overjoyed that she had not truly kissed Sir Alexander. A weight lifted from her overburdened conscience. She pushed it from her mind and scowled at the brothers.

"We did not mean to involve you, my lady," Alexander said.

"You seem to have an unfortunate habit of being places where you should not," Gabriel added. Alexander nodded in agreement.

She bristled at their judgment. "Well, pardon me for taking an interest in the safety of the barony," she huffed. "How was I to know what your intentions were? You gave me no reason to place my trust in either of you."

"I regret that," Gabriel replied, "but we had hoped not to draw anyone else into our plan. It complicates things." He looked at his brother. An intense, silent exchange passed between the brothers. They both turned back to Evelyn.

"Can you trust us now?" Alexander spoke, his winter eyes glowing with determination.

"I must ponder a while." She turned from them, walking into the meadow. The breeze flowed through the trees and down over the tall grasses, making them sway and dance. She sighed. Pushing past the shock of their revelation, her heart already knew the brothers were honorable men. The secrecy and deception made her uncomfortable. Still, Evelyn felt the bitter sting of betrayal at the knowledge they had switched places, confounding her emotions.

Evelyn looked up. A falcon glided across the blue sky, drifting over the glen and vanishing beyond the trees. She glanced over her shoulder. The brothers leaned against the fallen tree, watching her intently. Gabriel spoke to his brother, then approached her.

Oh lord, he is handsome. She swallowed. If she was not careful, she could lose her heart to him. Any woman could. What startled her was that fear did not pierce her heart at the idea of loving him.

Gabriel came to rest beside Evelyn. She met his eyes and saw the concern swimming in their depths. Inside, a wave of emotion threatened to overwhelm her. The words evaporated from her tongue as the silence descended upon them.

Should I trust him? Hate him? Her heart twisted at the indecision. She opened her mouth, hesitantly, then closed it again as she turned her face from him.

"I need you to trust us," he said. "We are on the same side, fighting the same battle." He reached his hand out, brushing the curl from her face to tuck it behind her ear.

Her heart fluttered at his touch. *How can I not trust him when he has shown me nothing but kindness?* His touch sent a jolt of pleasure through her body. He waited silently for her response.

"I want to trust you," she whispered. "I only wish I had known the truth about you both sooner." Her brow furrowed into a scowl. "You played games, shuffling me like a pawn."

"'Twas wrong of me. I humbly beg your pardon." His penitent response softened her.

It terrified Evelyn, the emotions this man made her feel. He awakened desires inside she had chosen to banish forever. Her focus remained on important things: the barony, her father, and freedom. She refused to admit she locked her heart away in a vain attempt to protect it.

She wanted to trust him. But opening herself to him meant sacrificing her freedom and independence. *A steep price to pay for love.* Damn her heart for betraying her. Evelyn pushed the jumbled emotions to the back of her mind. Right now, they had a duty to her father. She straightened, pulling herself to her full height.

"I am willing to put my faith in you both," she spoke evenly. "But I require complete honesty from this moment forward. I expect to be included, united until the end. Agreed?"

Evelyn sensed the hesitation from Gabriel, but she stood firm. All or nothing.

"Agreed," he said. "Under one condition. You take the directions we give you. No sneaking around on your own any more, for your own safety. Understood?"

She thought for a moment and conceded. "Aye."

Chapter Twelve

The brothers agreed to rendezvous at midnight that eve. Alexander took his leave while Gabriel escorted Evelyn home. The day grew warmer as the sun rose higher in the sky. Evelyn always enjoyed this time of year. She peeked at Gabriel riding beside her.

"Gabriel, would you switch back? Take your place as the shadow guardian again?"

He chuckled. "Why? Do you not enjoy having me around all the time?"

"Nay, well, I do," she stammered, "But, well..." She was unsure how to explain without betraying a confidence, so she spoke the truth, hoping he would understand. "Madeline, my cousin, has a tendre for Sir Alexander. It would be unfair to her for you to continue to impersonate him."

Gabriel's laughter startled her. "That would explain the strange looks she has been giving me. I thought maybe Alexander had slighted her, and she was out for his blood."

"Madeline is the sweetest lass alive." She defended her cousin, then added, "I only wish Sir Alexander would grant her a token of his favor." Evelyn nibbled on her lower lip, becoming lost in her own thoughts.

"Alexander has always been more serious than I," Gabriel explained, rubbing his stubbled chin. "Even as a child, he took his duties above and beyond what was asked of him. The perfect son he was, and it made me look like a hellion." He laughed at the memory. "Your cousin might be exactly what he needs to readjust his priorities."

Evelyn chuckled at the thought of them as boys. They seemed close now, but she was sure their different temperaments often clashed.

"In answer to your question," he said. "I will switch places with my brother tonight, if that is what you wish."

The statement made her heart flutter. There were benefits having Gabriel as the shadow guardian again. He was not bound by convention, allowing her to summon him at will. A man she desired, unhindered by the fear of being forced into marriage.

She noticed his arched brow as he glanced at her. A secret smile stole across her lips.

Gabriel gaped at Evelyn, who looked like she swiped her father's whisky from under his nose without getting caught. *What thoughts churn in that pretty head of hers?* An image of her flushed cheeks and kiss-swollen lips popped into his mind. He banished the seductive thought. She would never tell even if he asked politely. He scanned the path ahead, spying the stone wall through the trees.

She had been telling the truth about Madeline. He guessed it on his first day as his brother when she spoke to him and he brushed her off. He regretted his dismissal of her now. She had looked as though he had beaten her favorite puppy. He had been excited to see Evelyn, but such a poor excuse would not heal the slight he incurred against Madeline.

Evelyn had a blinding effect on him. Her request that he return to his duty as the shadow guardian was easy for him to acquiesce. Playing politics and pretending to be his brother were roles in which he wanted no part. Being stuffed inside the keep constricted him, almost worse than being imprisoned. The thought of returning to the shadows excited him.

It also granted him the freedom to see Evelyn whenever he wished. She was reserved when he flirted with her as Alexander, but she blossomed at his flirtations as the guardian. Her request sounded more appealing with every passing moment, making his anticipation soar.

Upon entering the postern gate, she reined her horse to a stop and dismounted. "I thank you for the lovely ride, Sir Alexander." She proffered a small curtsey.

He bowed with a sly wink and led the horses to the stables.

As night stole across the land, Alexander sat in his accustomed perch. He needed to talk to Gabriel, to switch back. The frustration built inside him. He missed the routine, the structure, and also a golden haired girl, who left the smell of lilacs trailing in her wake. His brow furrowed at the direction of his thoughts and redirected them, forcing them to remain focused on his duty.

The rustle of footsteps beneath the tree gave him pause. He strained to identify the man waiting below his hiding place. A few moments passed when another joined the first.

"Sir Richard, you had better have a good reason for this meeting," the first spoke.

"Inform the men to meet me after sunset on the morrow at the old mill in Charrington Point," Richard said his voice even and brimming with confidence.

"'Tis on the Scottish side of the border."

"Aye. Is that a problem?"

"Nay, not as long as we get paid."

"Good. I will provide the details then. Be there after dark, and try not to be late." Richard turned his back and walked away.

"What a prick," the man spat as he disappeared into the woods.

When he was positive both men were gone, Alexander climbed down from the tree. *Where is Gabriel?* He scaled the stone wall with ease, dropping into the garden on the other side.

The glimmer of light beamed from the lone lantern hanging by the gate. Darkness shrouded most of the garden. It was a risk coming into the keep like this, but he needed to speak to Gabriel post haste.

He emerged from behind a tall rose bush, stepping into the path of a young woman. Her startled shriek shattered the silence. His hand shot out, pulling her against him and slipping his hand over her mouth. The scent of lilacs hit him like a wave crashing on the shore...Madeline.

Alexander's lips brushed the shell of her ear. "I mean you no harm, Madeline. Do not scream."

Her struggling form pressed every curve against him. He groaned, grasping her hip to still her. His groin hardened, painfully aware of how much he desired her.

He shifted his hand slightly, brushing his fingertips over her lips. It felt natural holding her against him in such an intimate embrace. Every nerve in his body jumped to life.

"Who...Who are you?" she stammered, fear evident in her voice.

"Someone who cares for you." The words tumbled from his mouth as his lips grazed her jaw line. Her body melted into his. She turned her head, trying to look at him. His lips hovered above hers, her breath sweetly intoxicating. Every fiber of his being told him to resist, but reason was overcome by her heady scent and the feel of her soft body against his.

He kissed her. A fierce, passionate kiss that shook him to the core. He turned her in his arms and pulled her against him, threading his fingers into her silken mane. She whimpered against his lips.

"Och, Madeline," he murmured between kisses. "I have wanted to do that ever since I first laid eyes on you. You taste sweeter than I ever dreamed."

He felt her smile against his lips. Alexander kissed her one last time, and then pulled away. His hands lingered on her waist.

"I have to go," he said, breathless. Without another word he disappeared into the darkness, leaving a thoroughly kissed Madeline frozen with her fingers pressed to her lips.

Chapter Thirteen

The flicker of candlelight cast shadows along the corridor. Evelyn hesitated for a moment in front of Madeline's chamber door, and then knocked lightly. When no answer came, she pushed the door open to peer into the room. Madeline lounged in the chair by the fire, her gaze focused on the dancing flames.

"Madeline?" Evelyn approached her. "How fare you?" She put her hand on Madeline's shoulder.

Madeline startled at her touch. "Pray pardon me, Evey. I am lost in thought," she said, her gaze returning to the flames.

It was unlike her cousin to be awake this late. "What ails you?"

"Hmmm...oh, I am well. All is well," she mumbled, staring into the fire, held captive by a memory.

Evelyn cocked an eyebrow. Something had happened, and judging from the dreamy look in Madeline's eyes, it must have been good.

"Madeline, tell me what is on your mind." She placed her palms on her cousin's cheeks, forcing her to face her. Evelyn sank down onto her knees and searched her cousin's face. "I will not be denied. Speak."

"I went to the garden for a breath of air. A man stepped out of the shadows. He was dressed all in black with a deep hood pulled low, hiding his face. He"—she dropped her gaze, embarrassed—"kissed me. Och, Evey, you must think me wicked. I have no idea who he is, where he came from, or what he wanted, but I do know one thing. That kiss was divine." Her cheeks flushed a deep scarlet.

Evelyn bit her lip to keep from grinning. Inside elation consumed her because she knew who was dressed as the shadow guardian. *He kissed Madeline!* Now there was no doubt in her mind that Alexander had a strong attraction to Madeline. Strong enough for him to break free from his commitment to duty and take what he wanted. Her friend was smitten, well and truly lost.

"I do not believe you wicked at all." Evelyn stroked her cousin's cheek. "Merely human. Fret not. All will be well."

"But what about Sir Alexander." She sighed, leaning her cheek in her palm as Evelyn rose. "I feel horrible. Two men. Och, what am I to do?"

"It will all work out in the end, you will see," Evelyn said as she pulled the door closed behind her, leaving Madeline to divine the answers to life's mysteries in the flames.

Alexander stared at the stars, sparkling like gems in the dark curtain of the night. He returned to his perch after his blunder in the garden. He had been in such a hurry to speak with his brother he jeopardized them both, not to mention the mission. But no matter how hard he tried to punish himself, he could not conjure an ounce of regret for what had transpired in the garden.

The sweet smell of the blooms and Madeline blended together and wove its seductive tendrils into his mind. Although his identity remained hidden, she had been pliant and soft when he kissed her. She tasted like tea and honey. He remembered how breathless and lovely she looked, like a girl playing in a field of wildflowers. A lock of her golden hair had fallen from its mooring and framed her face. His insides twisted with longing. He wanted nothing more than to tell her who he was. Instead, he revealed the truth he kept locked away in his heart. He wanted her from the moment he first saw her.

Deny as he may to his brother, to Lady Evelyn, and even to himself, he was in love with Madeline. His promise to the Crown was the most important thing to him. But as the shadow guardian, the pressure of that promise faded. He finally understood the power, and allure, of anonymity.

A twig snapped to his right. *Gabriel.* Shaking off thoughts of Madeline and the kiss, he refocused his attention to the mission. The mask slid back into place.

"Alexander," Gabriel called softly from beneath him.

Alexander landed as soft as a leaf on the ground in front of his brother. "About time you showed up, Gabriel."

"I am, according to the hour, still early. Did something happen?"

"I overheard Richard and another man," Alexander replied. "There is another meeting on the morrow after dark. I have a feeling this will provide the proof we need to take the matter to the baron."

"Is that all?" Gabriel asked.

"I have a location and time. I tried to locate you inside the keep, but was"—he paused, struggling for the right words—"well, I was seen in the garden."

Gabriel's brows shot up. "Go to!" He shook his head in disbelief. "Who saw you?"

"I accidently stepped into the path of Lady Madeline," Alexander confessed.

"Lady Madeline?" Gabriel's jaw dropped. "What did you do?"

"Well, I had to stop her from alerting the guard, so I grabbed her," he explained. Alexander rubbed his hands over his face. "Then, I do not know what came over me. She felt so good in my arms. I kissed her." He shrugged his shoulders, admitting defeat. Gabriel would never let this moment pass without harassing him.

Gabriel's laughter bubbled out in cascading waves. He wiped the tears and clapped his hand on his Alexander's shoulder. "I am relieved you are human after all, dear brother. I thought for a while your heart had turned to stone."

"It pleases me to offer you amusement," Alexander ground out. "Can we get back to the task at hand?"

"Aye," Gabriel said. "By the by, Lady Evelyn requested that we switch roles, tonight."

Alexander hesitated for a moment before reaching up to remove the hood. He pulled it off and tossed it to Gabriel.

They traded garments, agreeing to meet the following evening to attend the next meeting hosted by Sir Richard.

Alexander knew they were close to the irrefutable proof they needed to bring the plot crashing down.

Evelyn felt the soft brush of fingertips as they traced a path over her jaw, down her neck, across her collarbone, burning a path between her breasts. The pressure of his lips on her neck made her ache. His tongue tasted her skin, his breath warm on the shell of her ear. He kissed his way up her jaw. Fingertips pulled down her shift, exposing a pert, rosy nipple. She gasped as his palm closed over her breast and he pinched her nipple, sending heat to her loins. He smiled against her mouth, and with renewed hunger, he kissed her again, deeper. She arched her body against him, forcing her breast into his hand, while the other cupped her face.

Her eyes fluttered open. Darkness flooded the room as the fire burned low in the hearth. Her dreams were becoming more vivid and frequent. They left her with a screaming longing she could not describe. Evelyn felt his presence beside her before she saw him.

"Gabriel."

"Aye. Did I wake you?" he asked. "You were thrashing and moaning in your sleep. I feared you were in the grip of a nightmare." He sat on her bed.

"Nay, but I was dreaming," she confessed, looking away.

"May I inquire what you were dreaming of?" His velvet voice dropping low.

"You."

He tensed at her response. She reached her hand up to push his cowl back and her shift slipped, exposing her shoulder. An inch lower and her breast would be bared. He swallowed, following the dip of the fabric with a glance. His tongue darted out to moisten his lips. Gabriel leaned toward her, stopping only when his breath caressed her cheek.

"What was I doing in this dream?" he whispered, causing her to shiver. His voice always had that effect on her.

"This." She cupped his face in her hands and kissed him. As

he deepened the kiss, her fingertips slid along his jaw and nestled into his thick hair.

She pulled him down atop her and sighed when he slipped his tongue into her mouth. Their tongues danced as his hands roamed her body.

He slid questing fingers down over her hip. Pinching the hem of her shift, he drew it up slowly, making lazy circles on the tender skin of her thigh. Delightful shivers raced through her as he caressed her skin. She reached between them, resting her hand on his chest. He stopped and brushed a light kiss across her mouth.

Evelyn pulled at the ties of his shirt. He groaned as her fingernails grazed his skin.

Deepening the kiss, her hands roamed his torso, his hips, and his backside. Evelyn savored every touch. He explored her with his tongue and his hands, sliding the shift up around her waist. His hands glided over her exposed thigh. She lifted her hips and leaned into him, wanting to get closer to feel more of him against her. His touch made her restless and ache for something she could not describe.

Her impatience made him chuckle. Gabriel slid his hand over the soft mound of her stomach and touched the curls framing the juncture of her thighs. His fingers slid lower, and she groaned when his fingertips touched her most intimate place. A shuddered breath escaped her lips. Sensation flooded her body as he stroked his fingers along her warm center.

"Gabriel," she whispered his name like a prayer. His finger slipped deeper into her. Her hands grasped his shoulder as he massaged, pushing against her walls. Her eyes closed as she arched against his palm. His thumb found the hidden nub and she bucked against him, her nails biting into his skin.

Overwhelmed at the sensation, the emotion, she moaned his name. Never had she been touched like this before. Now it was as though she was on fire, bursting into flames with every new caress. A cresting pressure built inside of her. Her grip on him tightened, afraid she would fall if she let go. He feathered kisses over her face, her jaw, and her lips. His presence surrounded her. She feared she would explode from the delicious onslaught.

He added a second finger, filling her even more. He curled his fingers and she ignited, consumed with pleasure. Her body tightened and pulsed around him. She whimpered as she collapsed, weightless. Evelyn lay there in wonder at the sensations that bombarded her. She had no idea being intimate with a man, with Gabriel, could feel so wonderful. Gabriel kissed her as he slipped his fingers from her body. He lay next to her, fully clothed, and watched her.

"What happened?" she murmured as she reached for him.

"I gave you pleasure," he replied.

"But you took none of your own?" she asked. "I might be a maiden, but I am not ignorant. You do not want me?"

"I do," he said, his voice strained.

"But..."

"I will not take you before we are wed." His hand idly stroked her hair.

"Wed?" Evelyn shot off the bed with a start, her breath catching in her chest. A familiar emotion reared its ugly head and threatened to choke her. She stared at him, horrified, not at the thought of marrying him, but at the thought of relinquishing her freedom.

"Aye," he said, his heart exposed with every word. "I love you, Evelyn. I want you to be my wife."

"Surely you jest." His face remained somber. She blundered on. "I will never marry." She said the words, knowing she would have to break that vow one day. *Why does his offer terrify me so?* She could not breathe, the walls closed in, threatening to confine her forever. "I think you should leave," she demanded, covering herself with the blanket.

"Evelyn, I..."

"Just go." She hoped she sounded strong, but inside, she was breaking apart.

"My apologies if I offended you." He slid out of reach and walked toward the door.

She glanced away as he disappeared out the balcony door.

Evelyn collapsed on the bed and curled into a ball, willing sleep to take her. As she wept, she knew dawn would break along with her heart.

Chapter Fourteen

Thrashing her legs, Evelyn kicked the covers off. Sleep evaded her since Gabriel left. *Why would he request my hand anyway?* She made herself quite clear about her views on marriage. She had a feeling that he was not the type of suitor her father had in mind. She had only placated her father with her promise to find a husband by summer's end. She would prove to her father that she knew what was best for her own life. Besides, Evelyn had known Gabriel for less than a month and he mentioned nothing of his past. He made her question herself, and that was the damnable misery of it. She had no idea what she wanted anymore.

Disgusted with herself and the whole tangled mess, she rose from the bed to greet the day. Her heart ached as well as her head. The walls bore down on her again. She decided to take a ride, feel the wind on her face. She approached the stables with quiet steps.

"Good morrow, my friend," she crooned as she neared her gelding. Jester gave a soft nicker in greeting. "Let us away," she murmured. Quickly grooming him, she tightened the saddle and fixed the bridle straps. Leading him into the courtyard, she scanned the people milling about tending to their daily routines. Sir Alexander was nowhere in sight.

She mounted her horse and kicked him into a trot, following the trail leading out the main gate. As she entered the forest, she pushed Jester into a canter, then veered into the trees toward the glen. Evelyn wove them through the thick trees, reveling in the wind on her face and the power of the animal beneath her. They broke into the opening and she urged him faster. His hooves thundered as the blood pounded in her ears.

A sudden movement in the woods to her right caught her attention, but before she could rein Jester to a stop, a large stag bounded across their path. The horse skidded to a halt, rearing up on his hind legs. The swift motion toppled her from the horse's back, and she landed in the grass with a solid thump. Her horse bolted, racing in the direction they had just come.

Evelyn gently flexed her limbs. Nothing seemed broken, but she would be sore. She blamed herself for she knew better than to ride at such a pace, even though it made her feel so good. Evelyn stood with an aching backside and bruised pride and limped toward home.

She prayed Gabriel had not witnessed her being thrown, that was if he had followed her at all. Part of her hoped he kept his distance today. The pain from the night before was too fresh. She sighed at the memory of his touch. She could not deny she wanted him in every way a woman desired a man. Since she had been offered a taste of pleasure, Evelyn wanted more. But in exchange, he wanted to bind her to him for eternity.

A quiet thought touched her mind. *Would it be that horrible?* He loved her. *But am I willing to take a chance?*

Evelyn kicked a decaying tree. A satisfying crack echoed through the woods. She wanted to scream or hit something, but her sword remained strapped to the saddle of her missing horse.

She wanted both him and her freedom. They worked well together. Evelyn was unable to shake the sinking feeling in her gut any marriage would position her at a severe disadvantage, as though it would put her beneath him instead of beside him. *A partnership. 'Tis what I crave.* She kicked another rotten tree, the dried wood splintering upon impact. She continued her slow pace.

Crack. The snapping of a branch echoed behind her. Spinning, she saw two riders emerge from the brush. Evelyn strained her eyes, trying to identify them. As they approached, a sudden dread snaked through her body at their blank expressions and cold, emotionless stares. They were unfamiliar to her, but she knew instinctively they meant to do her harm. Evelyn turned and ran, aware she would never outpace them without Jester.

Panting with exhaustion, she pushed through the trees, hoping to reach the road before they caught up. She screamed when one of the men grabbed her braid and slid to a stop. He twisted her hair in his meaty fist, forcing her to look up at him. The enormous man jerked her across the saddle in front of him with little effort. She flailed her legs, thrashing to attempt to slip from his grasp. When that failed, she tried to bite his thigh but his horse flew into canter. She stilled, knowing that a fall from the horse at this pace would likely break her neck. As she bobbed with the rhythm of the horse's gait, she wished she had heeded the advice Alexander so often provided.

Alexander strode across the courtyard in the direction of the stables. Perhaps, he would take a ride. The day seemed fair enough. His hand gripped the door handle when the sound of hoof beats behind him reached his ears. Pivoting, he jumped out of the path of Evelyn's gelding as it raced past him. He snatched the horse's reins. The winded beast heaved as white lathered sweat dripped from its flanks.

He shook his head. The foolhardy lass departed without an escort...again. His brow furrowed. Evelyn was an excellent horsewoman. *Something is amiss.* He passed the horse's reins to a page lingering outside the stables.

"Did you see Lady Evelyn leave?" he asked the bewildered boy.

"Aye, sir. Not long ago, out the main gates."

He retrieved his own horse and pushed the stallion into a run. Alexander prayed no harm had befallen her as he raced into the forest.

The new leaves danced on the slight breeze. Gabriel sat in the tree, his gaze fixed on Evelyn's balcony. He had not moved since he returned to his perch. He was a fool for not taking what she offered him. But his honor would not allow him to act on it.

Gabriel did not want her for one night. He wanted her forever.

He feared she would never relent. Somehow, he had to show her marriage did not mean the end of her freedom. With another man it might be, but with him, never. He refused to cage her free spirit. Her beauty was only enhanced by her wit and strength. He did not want to be her master, but her partner, a friend, and lover.

He sighed, leaning his head back against the tree. It dug into his skull, the pain a welcome distraction from the ache in his chest. The pounding of hooves broke his reverie. He glanced down to see Alexander approach the tree on horseback.

"Evelyn is missing," Alexander called out. "I need your help."

Without a word, Gabriel swung down from the tree and within moments retrieved his horse. The brothers disappeared into the forest searching for Lady Evelyn as fear stabbed through his heart.

The sunlight dissolved into twilight as they combed the forest. The hope she had lost her horse faded as the sun set, and the fear a worse fate had befallen her crept into their minds. They stopped to give their horses a chance to rest.

"Something is not right," Alexander said. "We should have found her by now."

"Shall we check the glen again? Perhaps she has already returned to the keep." Gabriel's voice held a sliver of hope.

"Gabriel, we have searched everywhere, even the village."

"We cannot just quit." He wheeled his horse around. "We must find her."

Alexander's hand closed on Gabriel's forearm. "I want to find her just as much as you do." His brilliant blue eyes were intense. "But we have prior obligations tonight. That meeting is the key."

Gabriel's heart sank. Alexander was right. They needed to hurry if they were to make it to the mill in time. Secretly, Gabriel prayed that they had somehow missed Evelyn and she was safe back at the keep. But the constant tug at his heart told him she was out there, scared and alone.

They headed in the direction of Charrington Point, hoping to get some answers.

In the keep, Richard stood next to the baron, itching to take his leave. The baron droned on about a plan for expanding the stables. Richard rolled his eyes, irritated with the man's shortsightedness. Glancing out the window, he noticed the sun had slipped past midday. It was going to be a long afternoon, and the anticipation for his evening plans spurred his ire.

"And right here," the baron commented, "can be converted to a storage building for the knight's equipment."

"Aye, my lord," Richard intoned; only halfheartedly paying attention.

A loud knock sounded and the chamber doors flung open. A startled page entered, his nervous energy pulsing with fear. He knelt before the baron.

"Forgive the intrusion, my lord, but we have distressing news." The words spilled from his lips in a jumbled heap. "Lady Evelyn has been kidnapped."

"What?" the baron roared, jumping to his feet. "Who dares commit an act so foul?"

"Lady Evelyn's horse returned rider-less," he stammered. "Not long after, a young lad arrived bearing a message, my lord."

"What did he say?"

"'If you want your daughter returned, a thousand gold pieces are the price of her safe return. Await further instructions.'"

"What? No name. Bloody cowards," the baron boomed.

Richard watched from the side as the scene unfolded before him. Things could not have gone better. He could make his move knowing with certainty Lady Evelyn was out of the way.

"My lord, do you believe the Scots took her?" he asked.

"Bloody bastards will pay if they did," the baron swore, slamming his fist on the table. "Send some men to investigate. I need answers, and now damn it!"

"I shall see to it personally, my lord," he bowed as he exited the room.

Richard closed the door behind him. He chuckled with fiendish delight. Everything was working according to his plan. Seizing his opportunity, Richard slipped out to meet with his men. He hoped they were treating Lady Evelyn well. Richard had every intention of seeing to her comfort. Personally.

Chapter Fifteen

Evelyn was blind. The stench of rotting grain assaulted her, making her gag against the dry cloth stuffed in her mouth. The strip securing the cloth smelled rancid. A heavy swatch of cloth was tied securely around her head, cutting her vision. She slumped in the chair to which she was bound with her hands leashed behind her back. She jerked on the bonds but they refused to loosen even a smidge. She shifted her legs. They were immobilized as well.

They took no chances this time; obviously her earlier actions taught them a lesson. The two thugs had underestimated her when they first snatched her up. As they watered the horses, Evelyn threw herself from the horse and charged into the woods, one of her captors hard on her heels. She had made it into the woods when he grabbed the back of her dress, ripping it. Her body slammed to the ground. He grabbed her calves, dragging her back to the horses. She kicked at him, clawing her way free from his grasp. The heel of her foot connected with his face. He reared back, swearing as blood gushed from his broken nose. She leapt to her feet when the other man grabbed her from behind and touched a blade to her throat. Evelyn froze at the cold steel against her skin.

She had watched the bloodied thug rise to his feet and pull a length of rope from his saddlebag. She followed his movements as he tied her hands together, pinching her skin. He tore a strip of cloth from her ruined gown. He split the cloth in two and covered her eyes with one then wrapped the other around her mouth, pinning her tongue down.

Effectively contained, they had returned to the horses and continued deeper into the Scots territory. Neither man spoke. After an hour of hanging over the horse like a sack of meal, the blood pounding in her head caused her to faint. Here she sat, bound, blindfolded, and gagged.

Evelyn listened, using the only senses she had available. She heard the soft gurgling of running water and smelled a musty blend of earth, wood, and grain. She tried to look around, but darkness met her, even through the thin material.

The definitive creak of a door hinge shattered the silence. Evelyn's heart raced and her ears perked waiting as the fear rose in her throat choking her.

"She is awake," a gruff voice boomed.

"I thank you, Vincent," a familiar voice replied. The cultured tones and sickening charm belonged to the one man she truly abhorred. *Richard!*

His footsteps echoed as he approached her. The thought of being alone with this man caused her stomach to churn. *The manipulative beast.* She would claw his heart out before she let him use her for his personal amusement.

Heat emanated from his hand when he fingered the cloth tied around her face, caressing her hair as he slipped the blindfold off. She jerked away from his touch. Her sight adjusted to the dim room. A lantern sat to her right on a small table. Richard towered over her, triumph emblazoned on his expression.

"So lovely for you to join us." He bared his teeth in a sinister smile. He slid the back of his hand along her jaw and across her cheek. She bit her tongue, refusing to betray how much his touch revolted her and how helpless she felt.

He circled behind her chair, his hands resting on her bare shoulders. Evelyn tensed, unable to suppress a shudder at the touch of his fingers on her flesh. She inhaled deeply, calming herself, and waited for the moment to strike.

"You cannot possibly fathom how long I have waited." His insistent fingertips nauseated her. "You are quite a valuable prize, you know? We could have made a powerful alliance, you and I, had you chosen to join me in marriage. Unfortunately—" he leaned close, whispering in her ear "—you never seemed to trust me. Quite a shame, that. It would have made my current plans superfluous." He tisked softly.

"Fear not, pet." His oily voice slid over her, making her ill.

"In a few days, you will have a choice to make. You can join me or suffer a fate worse than death." His grip tightened on her shoulder. "Aye, killing you would be merciful, far more than you deserve."

He released her, coming around to face her once again. Richard's eyes pierced her own. "Willing or not, I will have you, just as I had Rose. Your maid was a castoff trollop compared to you. She was pure practice, honing my touch for the things I plan to do to your flawless body. In the end, she was not strong enough to survive such attention. The wench even dragged your bloody Nora into it. I certainly hope the old hag enjoyed her foxglove-laced stew. Cannot have tongues wagging nonsense about my treachery, can I?"

The implications of his words sank in. Rose and Nora had both been killed at the hands of this madman. A wave of sadness washed over her at their memory. The sadness was overwhelmed by pure hatred. She murmured against the gag.

"Pardon? You have something in your mouth." He tugged the gag from her lips. She rubbed her mouth against her shoulder. His eyes were dark pools, the lantern light lost in their emotionless depths.

"Confident in your plans, are you?" she rasped, her voice hoarse.

"I will finally get what is due me."

"My father will see you hanged before he gives you anything."

His gaze narrowed. "Your father shall not survive the week, my dear. Tragically, he will meet his end at the hands of Scottish rebels. The very same, by the by, who kidnapped you." His grin mirrored his disgusting confidence. "I will then step into his place, being the loyal servant I am to the crown, and claim this barony."

She stared at him in horror. The gripping fear in her chest turned to anger as she narrowed her gaze. "You might as well kill me now. For if you let me live, I will stop you."

His bark of laughter echoed in the small room. "Poor delusional creature. You belong to me now." He traced a finger lower to the shredded bodice exposing the tops of her breasts. "All of you."

"Never," she swore, lunging at him against her bonds.

"Such fire and determination, even in the face of admitted defeat. I will have to tame you." Sir Richard grabbed a handful of her hair and snapped her head back, exposing her neck. His breath was hot on her skin as he drew closer, running his tongue over the pulse at her throat. His tongue, slick against her skin, made her stomach lurch.

"Mine," he murmured as his lips crushed hers.

Evelyn fought against her bonds. Her body writhed in anger as she struggled against his vicious assault. His hands gripped her head. She panicked, unsure of how to fight back. Then she heard the echo of Gabriel's voice in her head. *No such thing as a fair fight.* When his tongue touched her lips, she seized her opportunity and opened her mouth in invitation. He slipped his tongue inside.

Evelyn nearly vomited at the contact but lured him into deepening the kiss. Then she snapped her teeth down on his tongue, hard. The warm coppery taste of blood filled her mouth as she ripped the tip of his tongue off. Richard released her and reared back, screaming in agony.

"You bith!" he roared, glaring at her with his hand pressed to his mouth.

Evelyn sneered at him, a smile curving across her warm, bloodstained lips. She spit the severed chunk of his tongue on the dirt floor. Her lips curled back, exposing her teeth in a wicked grin.

Richard's arm swung, the back of his hand connecting with her face. A sharp, throbbing pain pulsed where his ring hit her cheek.

"You will pay dearly for that," he vowed, the words broken on his injured tongue. He strode from the room, slamming the door behind him. She heard his shouts and the flurry of commotion on the other side of the wooden door. Evelyn smiled, the blood cooling at the corners of her mouth.

His arrogance had given her a weapon against him. The taste

of his blood made her gag. She spit again, wiping her mouth on her shoulder. She needed to find a way out of here. Her bonds remained strong. In his haste, he had left the lantern. Her gaze darted around the room searching for something, anything that might help her escape, or at least tell her where she was. *Nothing.* She leaned her head back, praying someone noticed her absence. *Gabriel*, her heart called as a heavy sigh racked her body. What sickening, poetic justice to finally find someone who wanted her as she was, only to be stolen away by a man she truly hated.

Evelyn prayed, harder than she had ever prayed before in her life. The tears started to bubble, welling up from deep in her soul. *Nay.* She refused to cry. She needed to focus. Evelyn would never admit defeat, not until she released her last shuddering breath. A flicker of hope ignited deep inside. *Patience*, she told herself. An opportunity would present itself, but for now, all she could to do was wait for it.

Night settled over the land. Alexander and Gabriel observed from the shadows as two guards paced in front of the old mill. Both guards stood well over six feet and were built like stone garderobes.

They had to get closer to the mill. Watching Richard's arrival on horseback, Gabriel leaned toward his brother, anxious to see what information they could gather.

"Go around back," he whispered. "See if you can hear anything. I shall go up on the roof." With both of them in black and hooded, they blended easily into the shadows. He nodded to Alexander.

Gabriel climbed into the tree next to the building. He stopped when he reached a small gap at the peak of the roof. This angle afforded him a clear view into the mill. A fire burned in the hearth as a dozen men congregated inside.

He noticed a small door in the back corner, guarded by another devilishly large brute. His arms crossed as a surly scowl pinched his face. *Interesting.*

A shout pierced the low chatter of the group. The door swung open and Richard emerged holding a wad of bloodstained cloth to his mouth. Fascinated, Gabriel noted Richard's injured state and his anger. *What the devil happened to him?*

"That bitch deserves what is coming to her," he shouted, the words lisped and punctuated by the pain in his expression. The men scrambled from his path, providing him adequate space.

Gabriel watched amused and horrified at the sight of Richard. Obviously, someone in that room was unhappy with him.

The burly man closed the door, blocking it with his body. A stray thought made Gabriel wonder if he already knew who was being held in that room. All the men save one crossed to the other side of the building. He swore, unable to understand the muffled voices. Quietly he lowered himself onto the roof, stalking to the back side of the mill while searching for his brother.

The back of the mill was built into a hillside, buried by the earth. *A root cellar for keeping the grains cool.* He climbed down to inspect it. The stone connected with the earth, leaving no windows or doors he could see.

Gabriel spotted Alexander crouched beneath a window whose shutters were boarded. Alexander placed a finger to his lips, signaling silence. Gabriel knelt beside him. Both of them listened carefully, filtering the conversation to garner details.

"The two archers are to take their positions here and wait for the signal," a lisping, muddled voice silenced the men. "Choose the best two. The rest take positions among the crowd. The commotion surrounding tournament will provide the perfect cover."

Gabriel glanced at Alexander. They needed to get a better view of the men involved. Alexander stood and disappeared into the trees. Gabriel followed, stopping beside his brother once they reached a safe distance from the mill.

"I believe Evelyn is being held in there," Gabriel said.

"Are you sure?" Alexander asked, unconvinced.

"Nay. But there is a room in the back blocked by a massive guard. Richard exited that room cradling a bloody rag against his face."

"Let us set watch out front. Memorize the faces as they leave. We will need to be able to recognize them at the tournament." Alexander rubbed his chin. "I doubt they will try to move her this night. When they leave, we make our move."

Gabriel nodded, confident in his brother's ability to analyze the situation. They assumed positions and waited, their attention focused on the mill.

The men's voices seeped through the door. Evelyn strained to hear. Her racing heart slowed after Richard stormed from the room. Her lips twisted in a wry smile with the knowledge she had maimed the bastard. Her rage reduced to a simmer. When he returned, he would follow through on his threat. He would slowly torture her until her spirit broke. She had to escape.

The voices grew louder and then softened until silence met her ears. A key turned in the door. Hope fluttered in her breast. Perhaps they had come to move her.

Richard stepped through the doorway, approaching her cautiously, hatred glowing in his soulless eyes. *Has he changed his plans?* He removed the bloody rag from his lips.

"I am leaving you here for a few days." His swollen, injured tongue made his speech hard to understand. Flinching in pain, he continued. "When I return, I shall move you. And I will steal your desire to live."

He turned and walked away, stopping to give directions to the guard. "You and Samuel stay here and guard her. No one comes in or out. Give her no comforts. I shall return the day after next. Keep her alive."

The guard nodded as Richard left, the door closing behind him. Evelyn hung her head. This could not be the end. She struggled, fighting against the ropes as they cut into her wrists and ankles. She jerked hard the chair, and Evelyn toppled to the right, landing with a thud on the earthen floor. A plume of dust rose up, engulfing her.

The dust filled her lungs. Her eyes watered as she coughed and sputtered, trying to catch her breath. The door swung open and the big man glanced at her. Seeing her on the ground, he mumbled under his breath. He picked up the chair with her in it and set it to rights as though they weighed no more than a mug of ale. He turned to leave.

"Please," she whimpered as a cough shook her. "May I have something to drink?"

The man disappeared from the room. She waited for him to close the door, but when he returned, he held a mug. He tipped it to her lips, allowing her to sip the cooling liquid. She took a healthy swallow to wash the dirt and blood away. As he pulled the mug away, she met his enormous brown eyes.

"I thank you kindly."

He turned to leave, and she panicked. "Wait," she called, "What if I need to use the chamber pot?"

He looked at her. "Do you?"

"Nay, but I shall have to at some point." She pushed. "Can you at least free me from this chair? Surely you cannot expect me to escape this tiny room?"

His blank stare offered her no hope. He stalked from the room and closed the door behind him. The lock slid into place. Evelyn hung her head, cursing under her breath.

The tears rose again, choking her. Richard would rape her of that she had no doubts. Her thoughts turned to Gabriel and the last time she looked into his sapphire eyes. He had told her he loved her and wanted her for his bride. *What did I do? Shove him away with both hands.* A tear spilled onto her cheek. She would never feel his touch again. Never hear his velvet voice weave its dark magic on her. Her biggest regret was not entrusting him with her heart. Now, she would never have the chance to tell him she loved him with every fiber of her being.

Chapter Sixteen

The moonless night made it difficult to observe the mill. Gabriel and his brother kept vigil from the trees as a dozen men exited the building. He memorized every face, every detail, storing the information in the back of his mind. His heartbeat doubled when he saw Richard leave the mill and address the burly man at the door before mounting his horse to head south.

Gabriel peeked at his brother, but Alexander was already ahead of him. They pulled their hoods down and approached the mill, melding with the darkness. The large man stood sentry at the door of the mill, unaware of the brothers approaching him. Gabriel tossed a rock into the brush. The man stepped forward to investigate. Alexander materialized behind him with a sturdy board in his hands. He swung and it connected with the back of the man's skull. The brute collapsed to his knees, then onto his stomach, hitting the dirt and stone with a final thud.

"Check inside," Alexander whispered. He pulled a length of rope from his bag and bound the unconscious man's hands and feet.

Gabriel moved to the door and peered around its frame. He saw no one except the hulking counterpart to the unconscious man outside who sat with his back to the storeroom door, legs sprawled in front of him, nodding off. Gabriel decided luring him outside would be the safest way to effectively take him down. He whistled low and motioned to Alexander.

"Oi, get back here!" Gabriel shouted, as he pressed up against the wall next to the door. Alexander stood on the opposite side in the same manner. He took a quick peek into the room.

The man, clearly torn, shifted from foot to foot, attention bouncing between his assigned duty and the front door. Grunting, he lumbered toward them.

Both of them wielded their makeshift clubs high over their

heads. The man opened the door farther and stepped outside, spotting his unconscious partner on the ground.

"Samuel?" He moved toward the bound man. "What the bloody hell?" He scanned the dark trees. "Cowards!" Gabriel and Alexander simultaneously swung their clubs, one connecting with the thug's head and the other with his legs. He tumbled to the ground like a fallen oak.

"That was almost too easy," Alexander said with a grin as he tied up the second man. Gabriel plucked the keys from the man's belt and bounded into the mill. Reaching the door, he turned the key in the lock and pushed open the door.

Evelyn. With her limbs bound to the chair and her head slumped forward, the wild sable curls hiding her face, an aura of defeat surrounded her.

"Evelyn." He rushed to her side. She glanced up, the disbelief on her face shifting to joy.

"Gabriel, how did you find me?"

He noticed the blood caked to her jaw and neck, spilling down the front of her gown.

"Did that bastard harm you?" He palmed her cheek as he searched her face for injuries.

"Nay. He tried, but I fought back."

He remembered the bloody rag that Richard kept against his mouth. While his fists clenched at the thought of Richard kissing Evelyn, he smiled at her resourcefulness. Slipping his blade under the ropes, he freed her hands. She rubbed her wrists as he cut the ropes binding her ankles. She rose and threw herself into his arms. He gripped her tightly as they embraced, slow tremors wracked her body.

"Shh, hush, love. I have you," he murmured, stroking her hair. She trembled, her hands clutching him, pulling him tighter. "And I will never let you go."

Gabriel's warm embrace soothed Evelyn as she buried her

face in the folds of his tunic. She inhaled, reveling in the comfort his scent provided. He stroked her hair, every touch a consoling caress. When her tremors subsided, she pulled away, wanting to see his face. He held her shoulders as his gaze roamed over her, searching.

"Stop fussing over me," she said, her voice steady. "Truly, I am well." She must have looked a fright with her tangled hair and dirt streaked body, not to mention her dress, hanging in shreds, and the dried blood on her face and bodice. She touched her cheeks. "I need to wash my face."

Gabriel nodded and located a pitcher of water. She tore a strip of cloth from her ruined gown and dipped it in the liquid. He excused himself and slipped from the mill. Evelyn scrubbed Richard's blood from her skin as though it would poison her if she did not.

Gabriel and Alexander manhandled the two guards inside the mill. Dropping them in the room Evelyn had recently occupied, Gabriel nodded as Alexander locked it and pocketed the key.

"I will send some men to take care of them," Alexander said, nodding toward the room.

Evelyn's gaze fell on Gabriel. He watched her, concern marring his brow.

"Richard is planning to assassinate my father."

"I believe we know when," Gabriel said with a sidelong look at his brother. "And how."

"We need to inform the baron," Alexander said.

"Wait," Gabriel replied, holding his hand up. "Richard believes he has the upper hand by holding Evelyn hostage. He is unaware we know anything. We can use his overconfidence to our advantage."

"I still believe we should inform the baron his daughter is safe," Alexander said crossing his arms.

"I have an idea," Evelyn said. "But I require cooperation from you both."

"What do you have in mind?" Gabriel's brow rose in question.

"Alexander, inform my father of Richard's intentions," she began, slipping her ring off her finger. "Give this to my father to assure him of my safety and your loyalty, then impart our plan to him. I will hide in a safe location until the tournament begins, then when I appear, the surprise may cause Richard to let slip his hand. 'Tis imperative to keep my rescue a secret if we are to succeed."

"Where will you hide?" Alexander asked.

"In an old friend's cottage," Evelyn said. "There is no one there now."

"Nora?" Gabriel spoke softly.

"Aye, it is well hidden in the forest. I shall be safe there until the tournament."

"I will accompany you," Gabriel said, without looking at his brother. Alexander's mouth thinned in disapproval, but he said nothing.

"We should leave," Evelyn commented, pushing past the brothers. She stepped out into the night air, not realizing until that moment how that room suffocated her. She tipped her head back, letting the nighttime breeze whisper across her face.

When she glanced back at Gabriel, the brothers had already mounted. The destriers stomped with impatience, pawing at the ground. Gabriel stretched out his hand. She placed her palm in his. He pulled her effortlessly into the saddle. She leaned back against his chest, feeling him tense as her backside rubbed the front of his leggings. His sharp inhale made her chuckle.

"I crave your pardon."

"Behave, temptress," he whispered against her ear.

She shivered as his voice reverberated through her. His heat enveloped her as he prompted his horse into a walk behind Alexander's. The sway of the horse's pace lulled her to sleep against Gabriel's chest as exhaustion claimed her.

The soft footfalls of their horses surrounded the trio.

Gabriel felt Evelyn relax, her weight sagging against him. She had fallen asleep. He hoped the memories would not haunt her in her dreams. Relief swept over him at finding her safe, but seeing her in such a state tore at his heart. He wanted to know what Richard had said to her, done to her. Gabriel desired nothing more than the pleasure of hunting the bastard down and making him suffer. He allowed himself a wicked grin. He would take pleasure in torturing that man. But it would have to wait.

They continued, until Gabriel recognized the path to Nora's cottage. He reined his horse to a stop. His twin halted beside him as he nodded toward the path, steering his destrier deeper into the forest. Alexander gave a nod, turning his attention toward the south road.

Gabriel knew Alexander would find them once he spoke with the baron. At the moment, Evelyn required rest in a safe haven. They entered the glen where Nora's cottage was nestled.

He stopped in front of the abandoned building and slid from the horse's back, cradling a still slumbering Evelyn against his chest as he dismounted. He carried her into the cottage. As his vision adjusted to the dark room, Gabriel spotted a bed in the corner. Gently, he laid Evelyn on the bed, tucking a quilt around her. Fast asleep, she snuggled into the quilt, her sigh ruffling the wild curls on the pillow.

He returned to tend to his horse, putting him in a small enclosed pasture, then gathered an armload of firewood before returning to the cottage. Gabriel built a fire in the hearth, glancing at the bed where Evelyn slept.

The firelight danced across her sleeping form. His heart twisted. Even after all that had transpired, she retained her strength and beauty. *She is safe now.* Gabriel slumped in a chair next to the fire. He wanted to talk to her, reassure her of his feelings, that he still loved her. It tore him apart to see her wrestle with her decision to remain alone.

Somehow, he needed to assure her marriage to him would not mean the death of her independence, but the birth of a new freedom, one where she did not have to be alone. A partnership where they were equal. He would show her on the morrow.

Gabriel watched her, until sleep claimed him as well.

Alexander stopped outside the keep, pausing only to remove his cowl. He approached the gates.

"Who goes there?" a guard called out.

"'Tis I, Sir Alexander."

The guard shone his torchlight on Alexander. "You are free to enter."

Alexander walked inside the gates and tossed his reins to a nearby groom. He hurried to the great hall in search of the baron. His footsteps echoed in the silent corridors. He frowned as he knocked softly on the baron's private chambers. *No reply.* He pushed the door open.

The Baron of Rayne sat asleep in his chair, as a fire smoldered in the hearth.

"My lord," Alexander said, "I must speak with you."

The baron woke with a start, wide-eyed as the sleep dissipated. He looked as though he had aged a decade in single day.

"God's teeth where have you been! The bloody Scots have taken my daughter! We must prepare. We must find her!"

Alexander looked at him perplexed. "My lord, what are you talking about?"

"My daughter has disappeared! A messenger arrived with ransom demands. Sir Richard is convinced the Scots took her. He claims they have been gathering, preparing to invade the barony." He passed a hand over his face, dark smudges prominent beneath his eyes. "I know not what to believe. My daughter...I must find her."

Richard had planted the seed of discontent. "My lord," he spoke low and clear, "Your daughter is safe."

"What?" the baron sputtered. "Praise the saints! Where is she? I must see her."

"There is more."

The baron sat down, his countenance ablaze with hope.

"You have a traitor in your midst, my lord," he began. "Sir Richard has orchestrated a plot to have you assassinated and assume control of the barony. He is the one behind your daughter's disappearance."

The baron's face turned ashen. "I do not understand. Sir Richard has been in my service for years. What reason could he have to kill me or bring harm to my daughter?" He looked stricken, disbelief and betrayal etched on his hollowed cheeks.

"I saw him meeting with his conspirators this night," Alexander said. "Evelyn was there, kept as a captive."

"Are you positive?" the baron asked, his voice trembling.

"On my honor as a knight. That is all I can offer." Alexander hesitated for a moment before continuing. "My lord, I understand I am new to your service, but you must trust me. Your daughter gave me this to ensure you believe my story." He dropped the crested ring on the table beside the baron. After a moment staring at the ring, the baron met Alexander's gaze.

"We must call Richard in, let him face his charges."

"If I may be permitted to speak, my lord. I have a plan, one that may provide you with adequate proof of his guilt."

"I am listening," the baron replied, cocking his head. "What do you propose?"

Alexander sat next to the baron, sharing the details he had gathered from the night's events. The baron quietly absorbed the information. When Alexander finished formulating a plan, he rose to seek a few hours sleep before returning to Nora's cottage.

"Sir Alexander."

"Aye, my lord." He turned to face the baron.

"You have served me well. God grant you mercy."

Alexander nodded, slipping out the door. He prayed their plan would succeed.

Chapter Seventeen

The sound of birdsong woke Evelyn, sunlight spilling through the windows illuminating the small cottage. Evelyn admired the man sleeping in the chair a few feet from the bed. He sat slumped over, his head resting at an awkward angle, arms folded across his chest, rising and falling with every breath. It provided the opportunity to study his face, his features, without him being aware of it and returning the scrutiny.

A rough layer of scruff coated his strong jaw. The sweep of his hair brushed across his brow. Her hungry gaze devoured every detail of the handsome devil. She stood to brush the stray lock of hair away from his face. He never moved, remaining in a peaceful state of slumber.

Evelyn sat on the edge of the bed, her mind spinning. He had always been exceedingly tender with her. Since the day they met, he did nothing but care for her, about her. He never tried to control her. It was obvious he worried about her well-being. She nibbled on her lower lip and shook her head, unsure of where her heart was leading her.

"Something bothering you, love?" Gabriel's voice shattered her reverie. He remained in the same pose, his eyes still closed. The grin playing on his lips told her he probably had been awake for a while. Her cheeks warmed.

"Nay," she replied casually. Evelyn stood and walked around the cottage, searching for something to eat. Her stomach protested; it had been more than a day since her last meal. A glance around the cabin and at the empty shelves confirmed her fear. There was no food. Evelyn leaned against the table as her stomach loosed another growl, begging for sustenance.

Gabriel's footsteps echoed in the small room as he came up behind her.

"Hungry? One moment." Gabriel strode outside and returned carrying a satchel. He pulled out a large piece of bread and some cheese and handed them to Evelyn.

He disappeared out the door again. When Gabriel returned this time, he poured some ale from his flask into two mugs, and they sat at the small table to break their fast. Evelyn devoured most of what he had provided. He nibbled on a small portion, leaving the rest for her.

"Perhaps we should use our time today to hunt for some food," he commented. "Would you prefer fish or small game?"

"Fish sounds delicious," she replied. "There is a fishing hole in the stream over the ridge."

"Sounds like a wonderful way to spend the day."

Bound together by a common goal, the duo gathered supplies and wandered to the stream. Along the way, Evelyn picked herbs as she spotted them, tucking them safely into her basket.

"Where did you learn so much about plants?" Gabriel asked as he leaned against a tree while Evelyn gathered mint leaves.

"Nora specialized in their healing properties." She swallowed the emotion rising at the thought of the woman. "She was my friend and my mentor, and now she is gone." She coughed, dashing the tears away. "The knowledge she passed to me is all that remains."

Gabriel knelt beside her and placed his hand on her shoulder. "You miss her."

A tear slipped down her cheek. "Aye," she whispered. "She was the closest thing to a mother since my own died years ago."

Gabriel pulled her into his embrace. The basket toppled to the ground as she wrapped her arms around him. Burying her face against his chest, his strength comforted her. His hand tangled in her hair as he stroked the curls. Only peace resided in his arms. A heavy breath escaped her, and she felt lighter than she had in days.

"Let us catch some dinner, shall we?" he asked, brushing his thumb across her cheek to dry the tearstains.

They rose and walked down the path to a deep pool in the stream. The shadows of fish darted back and forth in the crisp waters.

"Care to make a wager, Gabriel?" she asked, a hint of tomfoolery springing from deep inside her.

"First one to catch five fish?" A sparkle gleamed in his blue eyes.

"Sounds fair."

"What do I win?" he asked, a smirk playing on his lips. He looked like a mischievous child bent on games.

"If you win," she clarified, and then a wild thought assailed her. "How about winner's choice?"

He took on a possessive look as her tongue dart out to moisten her lips. Evelyn could have sworn she heard a growl from deep in his throat.

"Deal," he said with confidence, kicking off his boots and stepping into the water.

Evelyn watched with amusement. He stood motionless in the water, his eyes darting back and forth, following the fish swimming around his feet. Well, she refused to allow him to best her. She slipped off her shoes and wrapped her skirt up between her legs forming makeshift leggings. Evelyn stepped into the cold water. After a few moments, the chill dimmed. She stood motionless, waiting...anticipating.

The cool water swirled around her calves. Evelyn glanced at Gabriel as she tucked her skirt around her legs. Every moment spent in his company was like a breath of highland air, exhilarating, refreshing, and heart-stopping.

Evelyn drew her hair to one side and twisted it into a ropelike strand, securing it as to not interfere with her quest. Though she focused with intent to win, she felt relaxed and free. Happy even.

She glanced up at Gabriel, who remained focused on the water at his feet. He reminded her of a hawk hunting a hare as he bent over, hands poised, ready to snatch a trout from the stream. Evelyn attempted to focus on her own quarry, but she frequently peeked at the hunter across from her.

She refocused on the water, waiting for a fish to cross her path. She spotted one and thrust her hands beneath the surface, plucking a decent-sized trout from the water. It splashed and squirmed in her hands, trying to escape, but she clung to it and turned to toss it onto the bank. Certain the fish remained safely on land, Evelyn resumed focus on the waters at her feet.

She slowly looked up at Gabriel, enough to ensure their gaze met. Catching his playful grin, she winked and looked down again, boasting without saying a word.

He searched for a fish. Swiftly, he struck, ripping the fish from the water. A grin split his lips as he tossed it to shore.

They continued like this for an hour. A triumph here, a miss there, splashing each other and gloating with every catch. Evelyn glanced at the shore where their fish lay. *Four and four.* This was the tiebreaker, the deciding moment.

"Looks as though we are even, love," he murmured. "Do you concede?"

"Never," she said, blowing a stray curl from her face. "I fully intend to take my prize and dance a merry jig all the way back to the cottage."

He watched the water, then stuck his hand in and pulled out his fifth fish. He held the wriggling trout above his head, the water sliding down his arms. Knowing she had been beaten, she stepped from the stream and turned to look at him with her hands on her hips.

"I concede," she said, throwing her hands up. Evelyn released her skirts from her belt, smoothing them with her hands.

"Are you cross with me?" Gabriel tossed the fish to the ground as he stepped from the stream.

"For winning?" she looked at him with amusement. "Hardly. It was a fair contest, and you clearly won. Unless you cheated, the fish may have liked the stink of your feet better than the sweet smell of my own."

His jaw dropped. "What a cheeky thing you are," he said. "And I shall have you know, my feet most certainly do not stink."

"Of course not." She smirked as she pulled her slippers on.

Gabriel picked up each fish and strung them on a line of rope. He dipped the fish into the water, rinsing the dirt and grass off. Their scales shimmered in the sunlight like gems. She rose from her seat on a rock, snatching up her basket of herbs.

"Shall we return to the cottage?" she asked, mesmerized by his shirt pulling tight across his chest as he slung the fish over his shoulder.

"After you, my lady," he bowed.

"You realize if you carry them like that you shall reek of fish," she tossed over her shoulder as she ascended the ridge.

"We already reek of fish. Does it matter?"

"I suppose you have a point."

An amiable silence grew between them as they meandered back to the cottage. *Content.* The fleeting thought surprised her. She glanced over her shoulder at Gabriel, who seemed transfixed by her swaying backside. She threw some extra roll into her hips, waiting for his reaction.

His gaze shot up to meet hers. Her breath caught as the sun shone through the trees, casting light and shadow across his face and highlighting his eyes, midnight blue with desire. Gorgeous and graceful, he stalked behind her. Evelyn was overwhelmed by the sensation that she was prey and he a ravenous predator.

His lips curled back in a wolfish smile. She winked; flirting with him was dangerous. She dared not push him too far. Even though she knew he would never press his advantage, a small part of her wanted him to take the initiative. Evelyn could not deny that she wanted him. Again, the question arose: *Am I willing to trade my freedom for a lifetime with him?* The thought gave her pause.

She hiked up her skirt a bit, allowing herself longer strides. When they entered the clearing in front of the cottage, she broke into a run. She heard his footfalls mirroring her own, their paces matched. She laughed as she looked over her shoulder to see him grinning.

As they passed the small pasture, Evelyn noticed another horse with Gabriel's stallion. Her focus shifted to the cottage where Alexander sat on a bench outside the door. Gabriel passed her and hung the fish from a hook next to the door.

"What news have you, brother?" Gabriel greeted him.

"I have spoken with your father," Alexander said, addressing Evelyn. "He is distraught at the knowledge of Richard's betrayal, but is willing to participate in our plan to draw him out. He is aware you are safe and will return on the morrow for the tournament."

Evelyn exhaled in relief. She did not want to cause her father undue concern.

"What plan have you devised?" she asked, looking from Alexander to Gabriel.

"When your father takes his seat for the tournament, I will escort you to his side," Alexander directed. "I shall remain with you both throughout the games."

"You are not participating?" she asked surprised.

"Performing my duty to protect you and the baron is my priority," he replied somberly. "'Tis my honor to do so."

She graced him with a toothy smile, admiring his loyalty. He nodded as his mouth quirked in a half smile.

"Gabriel, you must dress normally, but wear your hood. I need you to mingle with the crowds, staying in the background to search for anything out of the ordinary. Keep watch for two men with bows. Richard is going to use archers in his attempt to kill the baron."

"Two vantage points should help us locate them faster," Gabriel replied. "Keep a sharp lookout from your post, Alexander. They require a clear, direct path to the box. You would likely spot them first."

Alexander nodded.

"What do you want me to do?" Evelyn looked at the men.

"You need to be aware of Richard," Gabriel said. "If we succeed in stopping the archers, 'tis possible he will do something out of desperation."

"If he so much as twitches, let me know," Alexander added. "I will take him down."

Evelyn nodded. She always carried her dagger, so she could stop him if Alexander could not.

"It would be best if we waited in the woods behind the tournament field until they announce the baron's arrival,"

Alexander said.

"What am I to wear?" Evelyn glanced down at her ruined gown. "This is hardly suitable."

"Aye," Alexander began as he pulled a parcel from his bag. "Here you are. I asked a servant to pack you some fresh clothes."

"You are well prepared, are you not?" Evelyn said, taking the clothes from him. "I thank you kindly."

She carried the parcel into the cottage, leaving the brothers on the bench outside. Evelyn popped back out to grab the fish and returned inside to prepare the evening meal. She had to do something to quell the butterflies fluttering in her stomach.

When Evelyn took the fish into the cottage, Gabriel braced himself for Alexander's disapproval. When he did not speak, Gabriel looked at him in question.

"What?" Alexander asked, meeting his brother's puzzled expression.

"No snide remarks. No comments on how I should behave?" Gabriel asked, stunned.

"Nay. I realize now, Gabriel, you have everything under control."

Gabriel looked at his brother, dazed and utterly baffled. "You are not going to tell me to remain focused on the mission or tell me to shelve my interest in Evelyn?" he asked, skeptical.

Alexander held a level gaze with Gabriel. "I can see it. You love her. There is no point in denying it."

"I do love her and I want her to be my wife. But she refuses to marry anyone, even me."

"What is she afraid of?" Alexander asked with an arched eyebrow.

"Losing her freedom," Gabriel said. "She abhors the idea of her life being dictated by a man, any man."

"Then you will have to show her not all marriages have to be that way," Alexander replied. "It does not have to be about the man controlling the woman. It can be a partnership, with teamwork and compromise."

Gabriel blinked. "When did you become so enlightened, Alexander?"

"Do you not remember when we were children? Mother and father had a partnership in which they balanced each other. They complimented each other's strengths and weaknesses. Father never looked at Mother as though she was his property. He saw her for the treasure she was."

"I cannot believe I forgot that," Gabriel said in awe. "But you are absolutely right."

Alexander stood and grabbed his satchel. "I must return to the baron. I shall come for you on the morrow."

He retrieved his horse and mounted. Wheeling the destrier around, he called out. "Make me proud, brother." He loped off into the distance leaving Gabriel with a new mission.

The cottage smelled divine as the aroma of fish and fresh herbs filled the small building. While she was preparing the meal, she noticed a fresh loaf of bread and some cheese Alexander had brought. He truly was thoughtful. They would eat well tonight. The door opened and Gabriel entered the cottage.

"I hope you boys have an appetite," she said. "I have enough fish to feed us for two days." She looked at Gabriel, her happiness bubbling up.

"Alexander had to return," Gabriel began, "so it will only be the two of us."

Evelyn's smile never wavered. She had Gabriel all to herself again, and it would be their last night alone together. She wanted to savor it, commit it to memory. A twinge of pain nipped at her heart at the thought of parting from Gabriel. She pushed it away, focusing on the moment at hand.

Gabriel watched her, his face impassive, but she could tell he was thinking. She opened her mouth to inquire of his thoughts, when he spoke.

"Can I help you in any way?" he asked, stepping toward the fire where the fish simmered.

"You can remove the fish and place them here." She motioned to the platter and stepped back, allowing him space as he slid the steaming fish onto the table.

"It smells divine," he complimented, inhaling deeply.

They sat to indulge in their makeshift feast. Every bite tasted like heaven. Silence descended as they ate. Every few mouthfuls, she would look at Gabriel as he enjoyed his meal.

"These herbs are delicious." The words bubbled from his lips on a moan.

"They do compliment the fish well," she replied, drawing her fingertips into her mouth one by one.

She glanced at Gabriel, who stilled. He reached across the table to grasp her hand and drew it to his lips. His tongue darted out, swirling over her fingertip. Slowly, he moved from finger to finger, savoring the taste. Evelyn's eyes drifted shut as his lips encased her thumb, suckling and nipping the tender pad.

"Gabriel," she murmured, entranced by his sensual actions. His gaze locked with hers as she slipped her thumb from his mouth, gliding across the lower lip.

The temperature in the room increased. Everywhere Gabriel touched was set aflame. Evelyn took several deep breaths to steady the racing heart inside her chest.

"Your skin is sweet like honey," Gabriel whispered. He rubbed his fingers over her palm making her hand feel weightless.

"Gabriel," she murmured. "You...we cannot do this."

"Why not?" he asked, his earnest stare searching her. She had to look away before they weakened her resolve. "My sentiments have not changed."

Evelyn glanced back at him, his gaze intense, calm, and hungry.

"Perhaps they have." His velvet tone caused her to tingle with goose bumps. "After nearly losing you, perhaps I will concede to your conditions. For now."

"What conditions would those be?" She arched her brow, knowing he was placating her. Evelyn opened her mouth to ask him to clarify when he swiftly stood and dragged her to her feet. Her breath whooshed from her as she collided with his chest. He was tempting as sin. She took a deep breath.

Running her fingertips against his stubbled chin, she traced his jaw back to entwine her fingers in his soft mahogany locks. She pulled slightly and his head tilted back, exposing his throat. Her tongue touched his neck and his groan vibrated through her.

"Saints alive, woman. You will be the death of me." His voice dangerously low. "Have you done this before? With another lover?"

She pulled his chin down, so they were face to face.

"I have only ever wanted you, Gabriel," she whispered. "Heaven help me, but I do."

A smirk played on his mouth before he dipped his head, capturing her lips in a heady kiss. His teeth drew her lower lip into his mouth and he suckled. She wrapped her arms around him, pulling him closer. He deepened the kiss as his hands roamed over her shoulders, down her back, and cupped her bottom. She squealed against his mouth when he lifted her up. Her legs closed around his torso, fitting herself against him.

Too much in the way. Evelyn pulled at his shirt, dying to feel his heated skin.

"Take it off," she murmured between kisses.

He carried her to the small bed. When he laid her down, she pouted in disappointment. He stepped back, his silhouette highlighted by the fire. She watched, biting her lip as he slid the leggings over his hips, then pulled his tunic over his head. He wore no braies. *Of course not.* She smiled wickedly. Evelyn followed the curve of his muscles as they flexed beneath his skin and trailed her fingers over his abdomen, lower and lower until they disappeared in the curls surrounding his manhood.

Her brow arched. This was far from what she had imagined. His shaft jutted proudly from a nest of brown curls. She wrapped her fingers around it, curious and aroused.

"I cannot be held responsible for my actions if you continue to touch me like that, Princess," he ground between his teeth. Reaching out, he removed her searching fingers from his length and pulled her to her feet. "Later, you can touch me anywhere you would like. Right now, I want to see you. All of you."

He unlaced her gown. As he peeled the garments down, he pressed kisses to her exposed skin. His lips were hot on her flesh, feeding a desire deep inside. She shivered with delight. He slipped the dress and shift down over her hips and let them fall to the floor.

"Look at me," he whispered in her ear and stepped back. Her instincts were to cover herself with her hands or snatch her dress from the floor. He must have sensed her hesitation. "Nay." He took her hands in his, spreading her arms wide. "You are more beautiful than I ever dreamed."

The compliment brought heat to her cheeks as his touch tormented her with a delightful assault. His hand covered her hip, following the natural curve of her body up to brush his thumb across the tender swell of her breast. Gabriel pushed her hair back, his desire burning like a bonfire in his eyes.

Evelyn slid her hands over his muscled chest. Her body pulsed with awareness. The moment became overwhelmingly intimate. His thumb brushed across a nipple, sending sparks showering within her. His touch loosed a well of emotion deep inside, making her wet with longing. She pulled him down with her as she sat on the bed.

"Are you sure?"

"Aye. I want you," she said with a smile, and then kissed him. He slid her onto his lap, locking her in his embrace. His touch made her body ache and drove her insane with want. She could not get close enough. The brush of skin against skin was intoxicating. She shifted her position to straddle his lap, her thighs bracketing his, her breasts grazing his chest.

Gabriel groaned as his hands slid down her back. His wandering hand came to rest on her backside. He squeezed, eliciting a groan from her lips. Without warning, he slipped a finger lower, grazing her dampened cleft. She moaned and tilted her hips. His chuckle whispered across her mouth.

"Did you like that?" he murmured, stroking her nether lips with his fingertips.

Sweet torture. "I pray you..." she begged, panting.

He gathered her beneath him and stretched his body over hers with only a breath of air between them. He kissed her, then snaked his lips down her neck and over her breasts. Catching a nipple in his mouth, he suckled and nipped the tender peak. Evelyn arched against him, needing more. Her body trembled with anticipation as the kisses continued over her stomach. He paused, his mouth hovering over the junction of her thighs. He blew gently on the damp curls. She squirmed, nervous at the direction of his thoughts.

His playful smile eased her tension. Evelyn melted into the bed as his fingertips slid into the curls, finding a sensitive spot that made her arch of the bed. He slipped them deeper, delving between the tender folds. She gasped at the pleasant sensations that shot through her. He thrust his finger inside her as he pressed a kiss to her breast.

"Gabriel," she murmured against her hand, biting back a squeal of delight. Tracing her nipple with his tongue, he added another digit. She grasped his head, grazing her fingernails against his scalp, urging him on. He rocked his hand against her, his fingers stretching and filling her. "I beg of you, more."

He slipped his hand from her and captured her lips in an urgent kiss. Evelyn wound her hands in his hair as he hovered over her, nudging her knees apart with his own. His manhood touched her opening. He rubbed the head over her warm flesh, and then pushed inside her. She tensed.

"I do not want to hurt you, but..." he murmured between breaths.

"I trust you." She touched his cheek.

His lips brushed hers as he pushed deeper. She squeezed her eyes shut as the pressure built. With one thrust he was deep, filling her in a way she never imagined.

"Are you well?" he whispered hoarsely. He was holding back, trying to be gentle with her. Evelyn smiled at the tender gesture and nodded as the momentary pain gave way to the delightful surprise of being intimate.

He moved slowly at first, rocking his hips against hers. Pleasure sparked like a fire coming to life inside her. Her hands kneaded against his back, drawing him closer. Every movement brought less discomfort and more pleasure. She bucked against him and he moaned, increasing his tempo. His thrusts pushed her up, higher and higher into an oblivion of sensation. Their eyes met, and she kissed him. He returned the kiss with fervor, pillaging her mouth. Evelyn moaned with delight as he ravaged her.

Her body strained against him, reaching for the release only he could give her. Every motion sent her spiraling up into the clouds, until it peaked, catching her off guard. Her body trembled as her climax washed over her, wave after wave of pleasure ebbed through her, leaving her physically and emotionally sated.

Gabriel held her close, bringing them cheek to cheek as he gave in to his own release. His murmured whispers caressed her face. A sense of wonder came over her. It made sense to her now why intimacy was so powerful. It would be Gabriel, always him, who gave her such pleasure and treasured her so. Evelyn pressed a soft kiss against his beard roughened jaw. He sighed, looking at her, and kissed her soundly. Gabriel collapsed onto the bed beside her, his head propped on his hand as his leg draped over her thigh.

Evelyn lay there, contented, enjoying the gentle strokes of his hands through her hair, following it down over her breast. Warmth crept up her neck and filled her cheeks. He studied her naked body freely, caressing her everywhere. She turned to bury her face against his chest, when he tipped up her chin forcing her to look at him.

"A blush," Gabriel observed, touching her cheek. "You have no reason for embarrassment over a natural and beautiful experience."

"That was surprising and quite satisfying," she said with a smile.

"Would you care to try it again?" A sinful grin stole across his lips.

"So soon?" she squeaked in surprise.

"I shall give you a moment to catch your breath, of course."

His manhood grew hard inside of her, and she gasped.

"You are wicked."

"I know," he whispered as pressed a tender kiss to her mouth. "But you would have it no other way."

He smattered kisses along her jaw, pausing to nibble on her ear lobe. Whatever words formed on her lips died when her body ignited once again at his touch. As his hand drifted between them to palm her breast, she knew it a long, adventurous night lay ahead of them.

Chapter Eighteen

Evelyn woke to find herself draped across Gabriel. When she tried to move, his arms tightened around her. She blushed, glancing at the man who held her in his sleeping embrace.

Their bodies were tangled together, a blanket haphazardly draped over them. His hair feathered around his face, giving him an almost childlike innocence. Tenderness welling up, Evelyn caressed the bare skin of his torso. Her hands brushed over the scars scattered across his chest. As she ran her hand over his shoulder, Evelyn encountered a raised ridge just behind his arm.

"Got that one in France a few years ago." The rumble of his voice startled her.

Evelyn jerked her hand away, embarrassed to be caught fondling him as he slept. He was looking at her, a mischievous smile on his lips as he propped himself up on one elbow.

"What happened?"

"A man was unhappy with my sudden interest in his daughter," he replied nonchalantly.

She scowled at the thought of Gabriel being interested in another woman.

"I jest, Princess." A grin split his lips. "My brother and I were on the king's business when we were ambushed by raiders. It took months of training to regain the use of my arm."

A knock at the door made Evelyn jump. Gabriel leapt from the bed, not even bothering to pull the blanket around him. With his bare backside to her, he snatched up his sword and approached the door from the side and opened it.

"Good morrow, Gabriel," came a stern, familiar voice. With a gasp, Evelyn scrambled for the blanket and wrapped it around herself. Gabriel's posture relaxed as he stepped to the side, allowing his brother into the cottage. Alexander's gaze raked over his brother's nude body, then glimpsed Evelyn on the bed. He glanced away.

"I beg pardon, but you both need to dress, quickly." His voice resonated with calm detachment, but he searched the ceiling, a blush stealing across his cheeks. "We are to appear at the tournament before the opening ceremony. I shall wait outside." He bowed and strode from the cottage in haste. Evelyn chuckled at Alexander's obvious discomfort.

Gabriel closed the door, setting his sword aside for hose and boots. Evelyn's heart fluttered at the sight of him, gloriously naked and unashamed. Her hunger for him returned, acute and wild. They needed to make haste, but a secret part of her wanted to keep him naked in this cottage forever.

Alexander had both horses readied. Gabriel boosted Evelyn into the saddle and then swung himself up behind her. She nestled against him. He swallowed, beating down the hunger clawing at the recesses of his mind. One night did nothing to sate his desire for her. If anything, it increased tenfold. He hoped this day proceeded as planned. Ending the day with Richard's arse hanging from a rope and no casualties would count as a successful day.

His destrier tossed his head, impatient. The brothers nudged their horses onto the path, toward the tournament fields.

Alexander had arrived at an opportune, yet inconvenient, moment. Gabriel had been about to shower loving attention on Evelyn before his brother knocked. He grew hard, thinking of how the sunlight might play off her creamy skin as he made love to her in the morning light. He shook his head and focused on following Alexander's horse.

"Are you well?" Evelyn asked, tilting her head to look at him.

Gabriel grunted in response. He wanted her with an intensity that shocked him, but they had a mission to accomplish. Ending this would be the only way to ensure Evelyn's safety.

Alexander nudged his horse into a lope. Gabriel urged his

mount to follow suit, thankful for the change in pace. The faster they arrived at the fields the better. He had to get her off his lap; her backside grinding against his groin drove him to distraction.

They halted in the woods outside the rows of bright tournament banners. They dismounted and headed toward the crowds. Evelyn pulled her hood up to hide her face. Gabriel slipped his cowl down low. In a last second decision, he grabbed her wrist and crushed her against him, stealing a sweet kiss from her lips. She softened in his arms, and then groaned in disappointment as he pulled away.

"I love you," he whispered as he turned, darting toward the crowd gathering along the tree line.

Gabriel disappeared into the mass of spectators. She touched her lips and turned back to Alexander, who waited for her. They wove through the crowd toward the box where her father was already seated. They passed the colorful tents and banners of various knights. Alexander nodded to several, while keeping a hand on Evelyn's elbow and a steady pace.

She anticipated each spring tournament with excitement and joy. This year, however, trepidation and fear tainted her perception of the tournament, thanks to Richard. Straightening her spine and squaring her shoulders, Evelyn remained determined to stop his plan herself if she must.

While she remained hidden behind the baron's box, Alexander slipped into the stand behind the baron. Evelyn waited for his signal. Her father's voice boomed across the stands, echoing above the murmur of the people.

"This year, the spring tournament began under a dark cloud. As you all know, my daughter was kidnapped, taken to instill fear into the heart of the people." A chorus of boos and hisses met his statement. "But, I have received news that might rouse our spirits once again!"

Evelyn dropped the hood back and walked onto the

platform to take her place next to her father. The crowd rose, cheers echoing across the field. Richard, sitting several feet away, seemed less than pleased with her appearance. He offered a contemptible sneer as he slowly clapped. Her gaze narrowed on him, then she returned her attention to the crowd with a wave.

"As you can see, my good people," the baron spoke again. "Lady Evelyn has been restored to us!"

Her father embraced her, pulling her close. "I am glad you are safe, my child. I love you."

Emotion welled up inside her. She searched her father's careworn face. His bushy graying beard did nothing to hide the youthful glow in his eyes or the depth of his emotion. Strong and stout, her father was as able as any knight in his barony. He turned back to the crowd.

"Let the games commence!"

Evelyn sat to the right of her father. Alexander hovered behind and between her and her father. His posture informed her of his ability to counter any circumstance that may arise.

The knights lined up to begin the first joust. Evelyn waited with a shiver of anticipation. Though she focused her attention on the knights, she could not help but search the crowd for a dark cowl. The rumble of charging horses shook her as the first knights came hurtling toward each other.

The people around him thrummed with excitement. Gabriel kept to the perimeter of the masses, alert to everything. The sounds, colors, and constant movement created distraction everywhere. This was his gift, his specialty, blending into his surroundings, into the shadows, becoming invisible, and yet aware of everything. He detoured into the trees, searching the foliage for movement.

Gabriel observed the peasants, constantly shifting his line of sight. The cheers roared around him. He turned toward the baron's box. Gabriel barely made out the figures standing in the decorative enclosure. Confidence infused him at the sight of his brother behind Evelyn, guarding her with his life. The baron announced her safe return and the people cheered with elation. Signaling the beginning of the tournament, the sound of horses hooves pounding dirt rang through the cheers of the spectators as the first joust began.

Another rousing cheer erupted from the crowd. Gabriel surveyed the area. A flurry of movement caught his attention near one of the large trees. He moved with stealth and speed, circling to come upon the tree from behind.

Two men perched on a well concealed branch about six feet from the ground, clothed in greens and browns. He crept closer, slipping slipped up against the base of the trunk. Both men had bows drawn at the ready. Gabriel did not even glance in the direction of their target. He knew who was in their sights. With no time to warn his brother, Gabriel gave a bloodcurdling cry and lunged into the tree, just as the archers loosed their arrows.

The tournament was about to begin. Madeline lagged behind the rest of the spectators. She could hear the roar of the crowds at the baron's opening proclamation. She sighed. It was not proper for her to be late. With Evelyn missing, she had trouble sleeping and remaining focused for her mind raced with fear.

She walked toward the cluster of tents situated at the end of the field. The crowds huddled together watching the first set of knights prepare for the joust. Madeline glanced at the box where the baron was sitting. Next to him sat Evelyn.

Her heart nearly burst from her chest. Evelyn had returned and behind her stood Sir Alexander. Her breath caught at the sight of him. He was so handsome, standing there with his lips set in a firm frown. Her heart yearned to make him smile, to kiss his lips.

Her cheeks flamed, remembering her first kiss. The stranger

in the garden. She had confessed to no one save Evelyn. That kiss haunted her. Her only wish was it had been Sir Alexander, and not a hooded stranger, who kissed her with such fervor and passion. She trailed her hand against her throat wistfully. *If only.*

A strong arm pinned her against a muscled body as she was dragged toward the edge of the tents. *What could they possibly want with me?*

"Och lass, do not scream," a Scottish burr whispered in her ear, "I do not wish to harm you." He released the hand from her mouth.

She turned, attempting to see the man holding her.

"Angus!" she squealed as she threw her arms around his neck, hugging him. "I thought you were dead. You will be if they find you here. Why have you come? Och, you daft fool, you are trying to get yourself killed, are you not?"

"*Haud yer wheesht*, Kitten," he said attempting to calm her. "The clan to the north has asked for a treaty. They are wanting to marry the clans together in peace, so to speak." He looked at her, pleading with his deep green eyes.

"Och, surely you jest," her slight Scottish burr resonated. It only ever came out when she spoke to her brothers and when she grew agitated. At that moment, she was both.

"We need you to marry the eldest McLairn."

"Father sent me away to avoid that fate," she sputtered, shelving a hand on her hip. "I cannot just leave without word or explanation! And...and..." She became so flustered she felt her face heating.

"And you are in love with someone else, are you, Kitten?" he asked, tipping her chin up to meet his gaze.

She never had been a good liar, especially with Angus. He always knew when she was telling a tale. There was no hiding it from him.

"Aye," she sighed. He gathered her in a comforting embrace.

A loud shout pierced the din of the crowd followed by stampeding and pandemonium. Madeline turned to run toward the box, to Evelyn and Alexander. But a firm grip on her arm jerked her back as Angus pulled her in the opposite direction. He untied his horse from the tree and pulled her up into the saddle after him.

"Where are we going?" She shoved at him, trying to slide down off the horse.

"I do not ken what is happening here," he said over the screaming crowd, "but we are leaving, now."

"I have to tell them where I am going," she screamed at him, pounding her fists against his chest. "I cannot leave!"

Her words fell on deaf ears. She turned to look behind them, and in the distance, she watched Alexander charge into the woods. Her heart broke as they raced away from the man she loved and toward the Scottish border.

Alexander slipped a bow and quiver of arrows across his shoulders. The baron's private box gave him an unobstructed view. The tournament field lay directly before him, the crowds surrounding it, and the forest just behind them. The tree line, at a distance of less than fifty yards, provided the perfect cover for a bowman. He stood poised in the gap between Evelyn and the baron's chairs. Tension rippled through his body as he anticipated a strike. His hand slipped to the hilt of his sword. He leaned between the baron and Evelyn, his voice low.

"You both need to leave, now."

A soul shattering cry split the festive murmur of the crowd as the baron leaned toward Alexander. Two arrows zinged by, missing the baron by a breath, landing with a thud in the headrest of his chair. Alexander grabbed them both by the arms and pulled them low as a collective murmur rippled through the masses.

"Get down, stay down." Alexander glanced in the direction from which the arrows had come. A flurry of panic ruffled through the crowd as news of the assassination attempt spread. Chaos ensued, sending the crowd running from the field toward the safety of the keep. The mounted knights, who had been waiting for their turn in the joust, came to the aid of the baron, reining their horses around to encircle the box. As the crowd thinned, Alexander saw movement from the trees beyond the field.

"Protect the baron and Lady Evelyn," Alexander shouted, jumping over the railing. Sir Edward sat on his mount in front of the box, his sword drawn.

"Sir Edward," he called up to the knight who lifted the visor of his helm meeting Alexander's stare. "Detain Sir Richard." Sir Edward nodded.

Alexander darted across the field and into the tree line. He knew Gabriel was more than capable of handling himself in a scrap, but against how many? When he spotted his brother in the distance, he broke into a run, slipping the bow from his shoulder.

Gabriel stood beneath a large tree, facing two men with drawn swords. His sword lay on the ground behind them. Gabriel circled the two; they moved keeping their fronts to Gabe, lining up, one behind the other. The man in front swung his sword at Gabriel but caught only air when he feigned a lunge at the attacker. Stepping in, he drove his forehead into the man's face. The man grasped his shattered nose and collapsed to the ground, screaming in pain. Gabriel reached for his dagger as the second archer caught him from behind in a bear hug, pinning his knife hand to his side. Gabriel dropped his weight down. Using the man's momentum, he took a step forward, flipping the assailant over his shoulder and delivered a swift kick to the face, incapacitating him.

Alexander slowed his pace, about to call out to his brother when four men emerged from the receding crowd to approach Gabriel from behind. Alexander watched in mute horror as one of the men drew a dagger, sprinting at Gabriel with his weapon raised. Alexander screeched to a halt, deftly nocking, aiming, and releasing the arrow in one fluid movement.

"Gabriel!" Alexander called out. As his brother turned toward his voice, the arrow struck its intended target, causing the man to trip and fall towards Gabriel. The dagger caught Gabriel under his right arm and raked down his side all the way to his thigh. Reflexively throwing his left hip away from the knife, Gabriel crumbled, cradling the wound as he fell to the ground.

The remaining men turned toward Alexander. One of them charged with his sword aimed for Alexander's chest. Alexander parried to the right and stepped out, striking the man across the abdomen. As his opponent doubled over, he caught the back of his head with the pommel of his sword, dropping the attacker to the ground.

The next man dove at Alexander without hesitation, chopping his sword downward. Alexander moved in a drag to left. His sword sliced across the underside of the man's wrists. Alexander spun, his hilt jabbing into the man and knocking him to his knees. With a kick to the head, he turned his focus on the last man standing.

Their eyes locked and Alexander winked, sending the tall swordsman into a frenzied lunge, slashing his sword across Alexander's stomach. Alexander arched as he jumped back, the sharp tip grasping at his tunic. He circled around as the man pivoted. Alexander caught the next blow with his sword, the blades sliding together until their pommels struck. He pushed the man away and punched him in the face. With a last swift motion, Alexander spun, bringing the blade across his abdomen. He scraped the man from the sword with his boot.

Alexander dropped on his knees beside Gabriel, whose eyes were closed and breathing painfully shallow. He pulled the cloak from his shoulders and wrapped it around his twin's torso, binding the wound on his side. He needed to summon help before Gabriel lost any more blood.

Cradling his brother in his arms, he rose and strode toward the keep. The armor protecting his heart slipped away with every step. A drop of moisture bounced off Gabriel's pale cheek, then another. Alexander blinked and realized they were his own tears.

Chapter Nineteen

When Alexander disappeared into the forest, her hand flew to her throat. *Gabriel.* Evelyn attempted to persuade the knights to let her follow, but they remained steadfast in their orders to keep her safe with her father. She crossed her arms as her heart thundered in her chest. When she could take it no longer, she confronted Sir Edward. "I demand you let me find Sir Alexander!"

"I cannot allow you to leave for your own safety," he said, respectfully blocking her path.

"I will..." Her voice faltered as she glanced past Sir Edward. "Nay!" she screamed as she pushed her way past the knight. Alexander approached, his brother in his arms and his countenance filled with helplessness.

"Gabriel?" she whispered, reaching out to caress his pale cheek. He remained motionless. "Is he still alive?" she asked, looking into Alexander's sad blue eyes.

"Barely," he rasped, his voice breaking. "He...I do not know...do not let him die...please, God..."

A sob choked Evelyn as the tears welled up inside her. There had to be something they could...she...could do.

"Take him inside to my chamber, Alexander," she said, thrusting her chin in the air. He nodded, quickly carrying his brother inside the stone walls. She turned, meeting her father's quizzical gaze.

"Who was that, Evelyn?" the baron asked with concern.

"He is..." She stopped, astounded by the words forming on her tongue. "He is the man I love. Pardon me, Father, I need to save him." She caught the flabbergasted look on her father's face as she turned away.

Her heart ached as she picked up her skirts and ran toward the keep. Uncertain if Old Nora's lessons were sufficient, she knew she would damn well try everything she could to save

Gabriel's life.

She met one of the female servants at the door. "I saw Sir Alexander carry a man to your chamber," the servant said. "They were both covered in blood."

"We shall need every tonic and salve I have. I also require needle and thread, lots of clean bandages and rags, and hot water. Hurry now! Find Madeline. Tell her she is needed post haste."

The serving woman scurried to the kitchens to fetch the supplies while Evelyn bounded up the stairs, taking two at a time. She burst into her room as Alexander laid Gabriel on the bed.

Evelyn pushed past him. Gabriel's face and hands stood starkly white against the black fabric of his clothing.

"Aid me in removing his garments," she ordered. Alexander pulled out his dagger and cut the clothes from his brother's body. They rolled him onto his side, peeling the cloth from the long gash marring his side. The blood made it hard to judge how deep the cut was. She pressed the ruined fabric to the wound.

The servant returned, carrying the requested supplies. Alexander stepped back, allowing Evelyn to work. She cleaned the wound with fresh spring water. She asked Alexander to press a clean cloth to the gash as she threaded her needle. Carefully, she stitched, taking her time as Alexander kept pressure on the rest of the wound and the servant held a candle close. When she finished, Evelyn dressed it with healing salve and a fresh bandage. The servant took the ruined, bloody rags from the room, leaving Evelyn and Alexander alone. They gently rolled Gabriel onto his back and pulled a blanket up to cover his pale, naked flesh.

"Will he..." Alexander's unfinished question broke the silence.

"I know not," she replied honestly. "'Tis in the Lord's hands."

"I must take my leave," he said. "Will you stay with him?"

"Always," she replied softly as he left the room.

Evelyn sat next to the bed and monitored the shallow rise and fall of Gabriel's chest. She prayed when the tears splashed on her folded hands. If she lost him now...she pushed the thought away. He had to live. She had never prayed so hard in her entire life.

A soft knock woke Evelyn with a start. She must have drifted to sleep while keeping vigil over Gabriel. She leaned over him. Her stomach twisted in knots when she found his skin flushed with fever and hot to the touch.

"Come in," she called softly.

The serving woman slipped into the room. "I beg your pardon, my lady," she said. "I brought you some food, and Sir Alexander has returned to check on your patient."

"Aye, show him in Gwen, and God grant you mercy." She rose, brushing the wrinkles from her skirts. Alexander stepped into the room, his gaze falling on Gabriel asleep on the bed.

"Your father is asking questions." He looked at her pointedly. "I told him that he was my brother, but nothing more. He would like to see him."

Evelyn nodded. "Gabriel has not awakened yet. His breathing is still shallow, but 'tis the fever that causes me worry."

"I am confident in your abilities, my lady. Pardon, I must go," he said. Offering her a smile, he bowed and left the room.

Evelyn sat on the bed next to Gabriel. She laid her hand against his brow, burning to the touch. She tucked the blanket around him and prayed for the fever to pass quickly.

Her heart broke for she had been too proud to tell him the truth. She loved him, and fate now threatened to snatch him away. Evelyn leaned down, placing a kiss on his lips.

"Gabriel," she whispered. "Fight, return to me. I need you." A tear slipped from her lashes. Evelyn laid her head on his shoulder. She would break this fever, even if it broke her.

Alexander exited Evelyn's chambers, closing the door behind him. *Gabriel is still alive.* He took comfort in that knowledge. Evelyn would do everything in her power to nurse Gabriel back to health. He saw her love for his brother in every touch, every look. His heart ached, wishing he saw the same look from Madeline.

Absently, he wandered through the courtyard, hoping to catch a glimpse of her. He had not seen her in days. It was not like her to be separated from her cousin, especially as Evelyn had just *returned* from her ordeal. Alexander strode through the keep, checking every room for Madeline with growing concern.

Alexander returned to the gardens, having searched everywhere else. Deep in his heart, he knew that Madeline was gone. His chest tightened. Perhaps she traveled to the village or slipped out to gather more herbs for Evelyn. Fear seized him. *Has she been taken?* Sir Richard could have taken her as a substitute for Evelyn when his assassination plans failed.

After making a few inquiries around the keep, Alexander stumbled across one of the young knights who had seen Madeline at the tournament.

"A tall, brutish-looking man was speaking with her," the knight said. "Never seen him before. Looked like a Scot, if you ask me, but he blended in well enough with the rest of us. When the crowed scattered yesterday, he snatched her up on horseback and headed north."

"You are positive?" Alexander ground out, confused and concerned.

"For certain, sir," the knight replied. "I figured it was her lover come to whisk her away. She did not seem upset by his presence."

Alexander's hands tightened into fists with the sudden urge to pound the bastard into the ground. Then he remembered he never told Madeline of his affections or even pressed a suit for her hand. He had not approached her in that way except for when he was the shadow guardian, but obviously, she would not know it was him. He wiped a hand across his mouth. There was only one thing to do; he had to go after her.

With determined strides, Alexander approached the doors to the baron's presence chamber and knocked. He entered at the summons from within.

"Sir Alexander," he asked. "How fares your brother?"

"He has not awakened yet, my lord," he replied with a bow. "Lady Evelyn is caring for him closely, nursing him through the fever. There is still hope that he will recover."

"That is good news," the baron said, searching Alexander's face. "Is there something else you wish to discuss? You seem preoccupied with something other than your brother. Is it Richard?"

"Nay," Alexander said. "I am concerned for your niece, Madeline. No one has seen her since the commotion at the tournament. One of the knights saw her leave on horseback with an unfamiliar man and head north."

The baron sat up abruptly. "No one noticed her absence until now?" He shouted, slamming his fist down. He sighed. "I believe I am as much at fault as everyone else. We should have noticed sooner. Take whatever you need. Go, find her."

"I will, my lord," Alexander said, backing from the room.

"Oh, there is one thing you must know," the baron's voice echoed softly behind him.

Alexander turned to look at him.

"My wife, rest her soul, was the sister of Madeline's mother," he said. "Their roots lie in the Scottish soil. I took Madeline in when her mother passed. Her father and brothers still reside in the highlands."

Alexander flexed his fingers and his body tensed. He held no contempt for the Scots. They were entitled to their own land, their own country. *If rebels took Madeline, so help me God.*

"The last time I had word, their family was feuding with another northern clan," he said stroking his beard. "'Tis possible the rival clan tracked her here and took her as leverage."

"I must find her." He needed to move, to prepare. He had lost too much time already. "I do not want to leave my brother, but I know he is in good hands."

"Alexander, I know you care for Madeline and will do your

best to find her. I have faith in you."

He gave the baron a puzzled look. Was he so transparent in his affection for Madeline? Obviously, the baron, Evelyn, and Gabriel were more astute than he had assumed. His determination to find her doubled now he knew she was across the border.

"Any news of Richard?" the baron asked.

"Nay," Alexander replied. "After the escape, he disappeared without a trail. We will find him, my lord. There are knights out searching as we speak. I have doubled the guards until Richard is captured."

The baron nodded. "Go find Madeline. Bring her home safely."

Alexander stepped into the courtyard. He would wait until Gabriel recovered from the fever. Then he would track down the woman who had captured his heart.

Another sleepless night and long day passed before Evelyn saw any improvement in Gabriel's condition. The fever raged on as she remained helpless, despite her acquired skill.

Evelyn sat on the bed, pressing cool compresses to Gabriel's skin. She hummed while she cared for him, her wordless song calm and soothing. As she hummed, Evelyn's eyelids grew heavy. She stopped resisting the allure of sleep and curled next to Gabriel on the bed. Her hand lay on his chest, and she took comfort in the slow rhythm of his breathing. She rested, allowing sleep to claim her.

A soft touch smoothed across her cheek and over her hair. She smiled as the dream caught a hold of her. She snuggled deeper into the warmth beside her.

"Evelyn." Gabriel called to her. She shook her groggy head. "Evelyn." He called again. This time she cracked her eyes open.

"Gabriel?" she asked, connecting with a warm blue gaze. "You are awake?" She sat up quickly. "How fare you?" She touched his forehead. It was cool; the fever had gone leaving his skin damp and clammy.

"I feel like I died and went to heaven," he replied, as a smile touched his lips.

"You nearly did die," Evelyn said in a somber tone.

"It takes a lot more than a dagger to kill me," Gabriel said, attempting to sit up. The movement caused him to wince in pain. He laid down again.

"Rest." She stood and pulled the cover over him.

A knock sounded at the door. Evelyn turned to see her father enter the room.

"How does he fair?" Baron Rayne asked, who then noticed Gabriel was awake.

"I have been better, my lord," Gabriel replied.

The baron's gaze slid from Gabriel to Evelyn, then back again. "I see you have been keeping secrets again, Daughter."

"Father," Evelyn began. "This is Alexander's twin brother, Gabriel."

"I see," the baron replied, stroking the beard on his chin. "Where have you been hiding?"

"In the shadows, my lord. When my brother and I work together, one of us remains hidden as a guardian. It gives us a strategic advantage."

The baron nodded, turning to Evelyn. "How long have you known of Gabriel?"

"Several weeks, Father." She studied the tips of her slippers peeking from under her dress. Evelyn felt guilty at having kept his identity hidden from her father. "But I did not know they were twins until last week."

"Gra'mercy, Gabriel. For you and your brother's service my family." He walked to the door, glancing over his shoulder at Gabriel. "When you are well enough, I would like to speak with you, in private."

Evelyn swallowed convulsively. Gabriel seemed unaffected by her father's request.

"Aye, my lord."

"I shall inform your brother of your state. He is most anxious," the baron said as he turned, leaving Evelyn to tend to her patient.

Chapter Twenty

Four days after the fever broke, Gabriel could take it no longer. As much as he loved spending time with Evelyn, he could not stomach her bustling around him, clucking like a mother hen. It grated against his natural instincts to lie abed for so long.

Evelyn permitted him to rise from the bed the day before but allowed him to go no farther than the chair by the fire. He paced until his side and hip ached, forcing him to rest. He ate, slowly gaining back his strength. Gabriel decided he would attempt to speak with the baron that day.

His desire to be out of Evelyn's chamber was surpassed only by his desire to push everyone *else* out and take her to bed. Gabriel knew he was still too physically weak to act on it, but that did not stop his mind from wandering down such an enticing path.

When the servant came in with his clothes, he banished everyone, including Evelyn, from the room. Gabriel ate a small meal and washed himself. He stood gingerly, brushing his hand over the bandage wrapped around his side. Dressing himself would prove difficult. He slipped on braies and a night robe before he opened the door.

Evelyn stood outside, leaning against the wall. She brightened when she saw him. She walked past him into the room, gliding her hand across his stomach as she passed. The servant entered behind her and began tidying up the room.

"You know not what you do to me," he murmured, stealing quick a kiss. Her hand slipped beneath his robe, cupping him through his undergarments. His breath hitched at the contact.

"I know exactly what I do to you." With a wicked grin, she dropped her hand and took a step back as the servant turned with an arm full of dirty clothes. "Are you ready to speak with my father?"

He nodded. Taking her arm in his, he allowed her to lead

him to the baron's chambers. They took their time, allowing Gabriel to take slow steps and pace himself as not to overstrain his injury. Stopping outside the door, Gabriel drew Evelyn into his arms and pressed a loving kiss to her temple.

"Fret not, Princess," he said, brushing a curl from her face.

With a smile, he entered the chamber and closed the door behind him. He approached the desk where the Baron of Rayne sat reading a parchment. The baron glanced up as Gabriel proffered a slight bow.

"I am glad to see you are recovering," the baron spoke as he rose from his seat. "I pray you, take a seat." His gaze lingered on Gabriel, curiosity in his brown eyes. "You should know we captured what remained of your attackers, but Richard has fled."

"He escaped?" Gabriel swore under his breath.

"I believed it better for your recovery that you were not informed of the details until now," the baron replied.

Gabriel nodded, knowing the logic was sound, though it frustrated him to be kept in the dark. Knowing Richard escaped punishment for his deeds against Evelyn and her father made his hand itch for his blade.

"We will find him, my lord," Gabriel promised the baron, who nodded in agreement.

"Now." The Baron of Rayne's gaze collided with Gabriel's. "What are your intentions toward my daughter?"

"I love her," he said, speaking from his heart. "I would like to marry her, but I will not force her into something she does not want. I am asking for your blessing and for you to allow her to choose or deny me of her own free will."

"You know my daughter well, good sir," he acknowledged with a laugh. "Very well. You have my permission to marry her. He circled the desk. "If you can persuade her to have you," he said, reclaiming his chair.

A delighted grin curved his lips as he exited the Baron's presence chamber to find Evelyn waiting to lead him back upstairs to rest.

The next morning Evelyn entered her chamber to check on Gabriel. News of Madeline's disappearance spread fast, but by the time she had learned of it, Alexander had already left with a vow to bring her home. Since Gabriel's fever broke, she had been sleeping in her cousin's chamber. So much overwhelming emotion in such a short period of time exhausted Evelyn. This day she slept until nearly mid-day.

"Good day, my lady." Gabriel rose from his seat next to the hearth. He wore a robe and his cheeks were fresh with color.

"And to you," she said with a smile.

The servant popped her head in the door. "Your father wishes to speak with you," she said. Evelyn sighed. Butterflies fluttered in her stomach.

"Will you join me?" she asked, taking a few steps towards Gabriel.

"If that is your desire." He took her hand, and once again they took a leisurely walk to the baron's presence chamber.

Evelyn glanced at Gabriel. His face pinched with the discomfort of his injury, but when he met her gaze, she saw the spark of life in his blue eyes. He was a unique man, her Gabriel.

As they approached the baron's chambers, a guard held the door, allowing them to enter, Evelyn first then Gabriel following behind.

"You wished to see me, Father?" she asked. He rose from his seat and stood before her, taking her hand in his.

"I did, my dear." He took a breath as if searching for the right words. "I feared I had done you a great misdeed by raising you as I have, indulging you, teaching you as I would have a son." He lifted her chin. "I confess, I worried you would never truly find happiness in this life. The world we live in does not provide women the opportunities it does men." He sighed. "But I would raise you no other way. You are a strong, wise, and self-sufficient woman, and I am proud to call you my daughter."

"Gra'mercy, Father," she said, her eyes misting with tears as she kissed her father's cheek.

"I am granting you my blessing to do as you will," he said as he cupped her cheek in his hand. "You may choose not to marry, but I urge you to pray on these matters." He glanced at Gabriel over her shoulder. "You have the love of a good man; do not push him away out of fear. Accept love for what it is. A partnership can bring more freedom than a life alone."

Evelyn embraced her father once more before turning to Gabriel. He offered his arm and, when she took it, he led her from the room.

"Would you care for a stroll in the gardens?" Gabriel asked as they walked through the great hall.

"That would be lovely."

He led her outdoors into the bright spring sunshine. The flowers were in full bloom. She inhaled, savoring the aroma of the blossoms.

Gabriel halted, pulling her to a stop beside him as they reached the center of the garden.

"Find something you like?"

He tapped his finger on his chin. "I am not sure."

"You do not care for me now?"

"Nay," he replied. "I love you." Pulling her against him, he cradled her head in his hands.

"Evelyn, I want you in my life, and in my bed, from now until the day I die. I will never cage you or try to tame you. I will treasure the wild fire in your soul, the passion in your heart. You are a rare jewel, and I want everyone to see how brilliant you are."

Evelyn's jaw dropped at his declaration. Her heart swelled to bursting with love for this man.

"When I thought of my life without you in it, I could have died at that moment and not cared a whit." She placed her hand over his heart. "I was a fool not to realize you treated me with a respect and courtesy beyond your duty. You never stifled my freedom, only kept me safe. For that, I am eternally grateful. I love you, Gabriel, and I would be honored to be your wife."

A huge grin broke upon Gabriel's lips. Shifting her closer,

he kissed her, tender but insistent. She groaned when he deepened the kiss, her arms encircling his neck. He shuddered.

"Did I hurt you?" She pulled away.

"Only in a very good way, Princess," he said, grinding his hips against hers. "But it might be better for my recovery if we hold off a little while."

"That might be a good idea, my son." The baron's voice echoed behind them. He stood under the arbor, having obviously seen and heard their amorous confession. The heat rose in her cheeks, and she buried her face in Gabriel's tunic.

"You shall be married within a fortnight," the baron said as he turned to walk away. "My felicitations, and welcome to the family, Gabriel."

When the baron disappeared, Gabriel let out a long, low whistle. "Well, that was mortifying." He chuckled.

"It will not matter soon," she smiled wickedly at the thought of him in her bed every night.

He must have read her mind because his sensual smile mirrored her own. "Nay, it will not."

"Can you grant me one small request?" she asked, leaning her head on his chest and listening to his heartbeat.

"What would that be, Princess?"

"No more shadow guardian," she glanced up at him, tempting thoughts racing through her head. "Except, perhaps, on special occasions?"

Gabriel's head fell back as his laughter echoed in the garden.

"For you, my love, anything you desire."

"Let us go inside. Cook made fresh strawberry tarts. My favorite." Excitement bubbled in her voice. He chuckled as he led her toward the kitchen.

"Aye, Princess. As you wish."

Chapter Twenty-One

Several Months Later

The autumn weather had turned brisk. Evelyn stood on her balcony looking down into her slowly browning garden. She let the chilly breeze catch the tendrils of hair blowing them across her face.

"You should not be out in this cold, Princess," a velvet voice wafted from the shadows beside her. A darkly clad figure stepped from the ledge to the balcony. He sauntered slowly toward her, his dark cowl pulled low.

"You promised."

"But this is a special occasion," he whispered as he pulled her into his arms. "We have located Richard."

Her blood chilled at the name. He needed to be captured and brought to justice, but deep inside, she wished someone else could do it. She feared for her husband's safety.

The fabric slid through her fingers as she touched the hood. "Be careful, my love," she whispered. "We need you home safe."

"We?"

"Aye," she replied, placing his hand on her stomach. "We."

Even though she could not see his face, she knew he was grinning. He kissed her with tenderness. Her passion rose from deep inside as she returned the kiss.

"I will return home soon." He pressed a soft kiss to her lips one last time and disappeared into the moonless night.

The gaping darkness consumed him. Richard ran, branches slapping his torso and face as he raced through the forest. He could hear them coming. They were hunting him.

He stumbled over a large fallen branch and the wind whooshed from his lungs as he slammed into the ground. Richard scrambled to his feet, his heart thundering in his chest.

The moonless night provided him no favors. He blindly pushed through the forest, unsure of his direction. A figure stepped out in front of him, causing him to stumble. The figure wore a hood matching his dark garb. The man took a menacing step toward him. Richard backed up and tripped over a stone, his backside connecting with the ground. He scooted away from the hooded figure until his back collided with something.

Richard glanced over his shoulder to see what blocked his escape. It was a pair of legs, connected to a mirror image of the man before him.

"Who are you?" he shouted, shooting evil glares from one to the other. "What do you want from me?"

"Richard Langley, you are under arrest for the attempted assassination of James Montgomery, Baron of Rayne," the first shrouded figure spoke.

"And for threatening my wife, you bloody bastard," the one behind him swore. "How fares your tongue?"

Richard's eyes grew wide. *How did they know where to find me?*

"You have the wrong man."

"I do not think so," the first man replied confidently. "Take him, Gabe."

The man behind him grabbed him by the arms, jerking him to his feet. "You will never get away with this."

"We could always have an accident on the way back to your trial," the one holding him said. "Just a slip, and oh look, you fell on my dagger."

"Gabe," the first man scolded. "Although that idea might save us an immeasurable amount of time and trouble, I believe keeping him alive might have more merit for justice. Although, I did promise to relieve him of his hands if he ever touched Lady Evelyn again."

"Nay! You cannot do this to me," Richard screamed as they bound his wrists and hauled him away.

"Would you gag him as well?" the somber one asked. "The

sound of his voice is making my head pound."

"With pleasure." The other man stopped to pull a scrap of fabric from his bag and tied it across Richard's mouth.

"Ah, the sweet sound of silence," the man said, dragging him into the night toward an unfortunate end.

The End

ABOUT THE AUTHOR

Kirsten S. Blacketer is a multi-published indie author of both historical and contemporary romance. When she's not writing, she homeschools her two children and enjoys time with her family. In those moments of freedom, she devours romance novels while sipping a glass of wine. Age has only shown her that writing villains can be just as fun as heroes. Her next life goals are to write a New York Times Bestseller and one day have Adam Driver play a starring role in a film version of one of her books. A girl can dream, right?

Read more at **http://kirstensblacketer.com.**

ALSO WRITES AS JEN BRADLEE

OTHER BOOKS BY KIRSTEN S. BLACKETER

CRAVING 1985 SERIES

When I Found You
Can't Fight This Feeling
She Gives Love a Bad Name
Owner of a Lonely Heart
Just What I Needed

HISTORICAL

An Irresistible Shadow
A Shadow's Kiss
Mississippi Moonshine
Deceiving the Earl
Jewel of Winter
At Winter's Demand
Under Winter's Control
Seducing Winter's Gentleman
Stealing the Widow's Heart
Seduction on the Alpine Express
Temptation on the Alpine Express

CONTEMPORARY

A Lockdown Love Affair
A Holiday Love Affair
Mistletoe and Mistakes
Confessions of a Fangirl
Confessions of a Gamer Girl
Confessions of a Glamour Girl

FANTASY/FAIRYTALE

Curse of the Huntsman's Jewel
The Huntsman's Revenge

PIRATES AND PERSUASION

Queen Takes Hook